"This guy is here to shut down the shelter."

"No, I'm not. If I could speak for myself…" Blake shot Charlie a pointed look before turning back to Rachel.

"Oh…" The shelter manager's gaze darted between the two of them, then her eyes lit up. *"Ohh."*

"No way." Charlie waved her hand erratically at Rachel. "It's not what you're thinking."

Now he was the one confused. "Ladies?"

"Can you please focus on the fact that this man is trying to shut down Paradise Paws? At *Christmas*?" Charlie's ire returned—this time directed back at Blake.

"I'm *not* shutting down the shelter." He held up both hands. "There's a very generous offer on the table, one that, in my opinion, Paradise Paws would be wise to take."

"That's just it." Charlie twisted in her seat to face him. "No one asked for your opinion."

"I think that's up to Ms. Rose to decide." The sooner he landed this deal, the sooner he could switch gears and further pursue the real reason he was here.

To get to know his niece.

Betsy St. Amant is the author of over twenty romance novels and novellas. She resides in North Louisiana with her hubby, two daughters, an impressive stash of coffee mugs and one furry schnauzer-toddler. Betsy has a BA in communications and a deep-rooted passion for seeing women restored to truth. When she's not composing her next book or trying to prove unicorns are real, Betsy can be found somewhere in the vicinity of an iced coffee. She writes frequently for www.ibelieve.com, a devotional site for women.

Books by Betsy St. Amant

Love Inspired

Visit the Author Profile page at LoveInspired.com for more titles.

Second Chance Christmas

Betsy St. Amant

LOVE INSPIRED
INSPIRATIONAL ROMANCE

LOVE INSPIRED®

INSPIRATIONAL ROMANCE

Recycling programs
for this product may
not exist in your area.

ISBN-13: 978-1-335-58529-5

Second Chance Christmas

Copyright © 2022 by Betsy St. Amant

For questions and comments about the quality of this book, please contact us at CustomerService@Harlequin.com.

Love Inspired
22 Adelaide St. West, 41st Floor
Toronto, Ontario M5H 4E3, Canada
www.LoveInspired.com

Printed in U.S.A.

Learn to do well; seek judgment,
relieve the oppressed, judge the fatherless,
plead for the widow.
            —*Isaiah* 1:17

To my daddy—
thanks for jump-starting my love of dogs by coming home
with two puppies tucked under your denim jacket.

Acknowledgments

No author is an island! I'm so grateful to get to
repeatedly work with my agent of nearly fifteen years,
Tamela Hancock Murray of the Steve Laube Agency, who
blesses me with her professional insight and wisdom. And
I'm incredibly blessed to have editor Emily Rodmell on my
team, who always knows just what the story needs to take
it to the next level.

Special thanks to Phil Martinez for answering my endless
questions about the CASA program and enduring my
frequent exclamations of "Oh! And then what if…"; and to
CASA program coordinator Patricia Anderson-Alicea, for
providing so much quality information through Phil. Any
errors in expression are mine alone.

As always, any time I write a novel, there are those
inevitable days of Looming Deadline, where my family
must scavenge for food and endure a slightly more uptight
version of Wife/Mom. Thanks, family, for liking frozen
pizza. You guys are the best.

A big thank-you to the family dog, Cooper—our own
miniature schnauzer, who demanded a cameo in this
story—for being ridiculously cute and so generous with
his "shuggies" and "woobies."

To all my friends who pray for me through each contract,
writing session, revision and deadline, and who ask
how it's going and are truly interested in the answer—
thank you. You know who you are.

And to all my readers who buy my books and send
encouraging emails—you guys are amazing! I couldn't do
this whole writing gig without you.

Last but never least, I'm so grateful to the Lord Jesus Christ
for allowing me in His sovereignty to do what I love—
share His goodness through the written word.

Chapter One

Charlie Bussey might not have a lot of men fighting over her, but after this last batch of peanut butter cake balls, a bunch of dogs sure would be.

She pulled the baking sheet from the oven of the community kitchen where she created all her unique concoctions for Flour Power and fanned an oven mitt over the little Santa hat–shaped dog treats. "Perfect." This time, she'd added enough flour to keep the consistency firmer. The last batch had ended up in the trash, much to the dismay of her adopted miniature schnauzer, Cooper.

"Do you ever taste them?" Nadia, a teenager from the group foster home who was taking her turn shadowing Charlie's pop-up business, pulled her dark braid over her shoulder as she stepped out of the way of the hot tray.

"Of course." Charlie set the tray on the rack and reached for a nearby spatula.

Barely masked judgment clouded Nadia's expression.

Charlie waved the oven mitt at her and rolled her eyes. "It's mostly peanut butter—not actual dog food."

"Right…"

"Very funny." She scooped one up and offered it to the aloof teenager. "Try it."

"No, thanks. I had kibble for lunch."

"Okay, that *was* funny." Charlie lowered the spatula. "You know, Tori always helps me taste test." Tori, the newest teen in the group home, had been catching up on a math lesson with the house mother when they left, or she'd have tagged along. If anyone had the patience to deal with both teenagers *and* math tutoring, it was Gretchen Jolie. She planned to drop Tori by the kitchen to meet up with Charlie before they left to make their deliveries.

"Of course Tori helps." Nadia rolled her eyes. "She's thirteen and a giant—"

"Careful," Charlie warned, gentling the admonition with a smile. She plated the dog cookies and dumped the baking sheet in the industrial sink. Tori and Nadia's big sis/little sis dynamic was still developing, but the roots were there. Sixteen-year-old Nadia had been in the group home under the care of Art and Gretchen Jolie for over a year, while Tori had transitioned from a temporary-placement foster home just four months ago—hence the need for her to have a Court Appointed Special Advocate. Charlie had jumped at the opportunity to represent the sweet girl in court and be a voice for her well-being while she was in the system. And though there seemed to be an initial element of jealousy over the attention Tori got for being younger, Charlie knew the protective instincts Nadia attempted to hide under the guise of annoyance ran deep.

Charlie moved past Nadia to the stainless-steel refrigerator. Her time volunteering at the group foster home never left Charlie bored—maybe left her with a few extra stress wrinkles in her forehead, but never bored. When Nadia first arrived, she'd refused to give Charlie the time of day—until Charlie presented the angsty teen with a dual pack of high-quality nail polish. One lip liner and an eyelash curler later, they'd eased into a genuine relationship of mentor/mentee.

Tori, however, had taken to Charlie from the moment she'd arrived. Much less hardened, Tori was as eager for love as Nadia was to distrust it.

Charlie clicked off the oven. "Hand me that bakery box, will you? Our hour is almost up."

She could only afford brief sessions in the community kitchen, even though it was already discounted in rental fees because of her being a local small business. Which worked perfectly for Charlie—she hated handouts. Ever since her dad had abandoned their family when she was only four, and her substance-abusing mom decided about six years later that raising a kid alone cramped her lifestyle, Charlie had become all too familiar with pity. She'd gotten word from her prior caseworker that her parents had both passed away sometime during Charlie's teen years. Now she was twenty-nine, with her own business. Thanks to her foster parents, Art and Gretchen, she'd overcome all the odds.

And those odds were the ones she was determined to help Nadia, Tori and the other girls hurdle right on over, too. One Santa hat–shaped peanut butter dog treat at a time, if it came to it.

The kitchen door swung open, and thirteen-year-old Tori strode inside, her long honey-blond ponytail dangling beneath a winter hat. "Finally! Math is done."

Charlie stepped over and waved to Gretchen from the

door before the house mother pulled away in her van. "I bet Mama Gretchen feels the exact same relief."

Tori sniffed the air, much like Charlie's dog, Cooper. "I smell peanut butter. Are these cookies people-friendly, too?"

"Depends on who you ask." Nadia shot Charlie a pointed look.

"These are safe to taste test, but you probably don't want to chow down as a snack." Charlie grinned. "Now, let's get these ready to go."

Together, the three of them began loading the freshly baked treats into the bakery box. "Where are you selling these this week?" Nadia asked.

Charlie gently laid a sheet of parchment paper on top of the first layer of peanut butter hats before starting to stack the second. "I'm taking one batch to the animal shelter."

"*Duh,*" Nadia and Tori said at the same time.

Charlie scooted two treats closer together to make room for the last one. "You know, if I could adopt all the dogs there myself, I would."

Nadia wadded up the scraps of parchment paper they hadn't used. "Why don't you?"

"My apartment only lets me have one dog at a time. Plus, dogs need shots and food and vet checks… It adds up quick."

Nadia tossed the paper into the nearby wastebasket. "You could always marry rich."

Charlie winced. "Twenty-nine and single. Don't re-mind me."

"Was your ex-boyfriend rich?" Nadia crossed her slim arms over her middle.

Charlie slowly folded over the lid of the box, avoiding the teen's knowing gaze. "What ex-boyfriend?" Her heart thudded so loudly she was sure it'd give her away.

"Oh, you have an ex?" Tori snatched a peanut butter cookie from the box before Charlie could finish closing the lid and nibbled the end of the dog treat.

Nadia rolled her eyes at Tori before turning back to Charlie. "The guy who broke your heart, the one who got away—whatever you want to call him."

Oh, there were plenty of things she could call Blake, but none quite appropriate for teen ears.

"You used to talk about him a lot, especially to Mama Gretchen when you didn't think we were listening," Nadia pressed. "You're not as subtle as you think you are."

"More like you guys are sneakier than I thought you were." Charlie snorted.

"This sounds like a romance novel." Tori leaned in across the counter, eyes wide with interest.

"Wait a second. How do you know about romance novels?" Charlie arched her eyebrow at the younger teen.

"My old foster mom liked to read them. They were always lying all over the house." Tori shrugged. "I got bored."

"Who cares? Tell us more about the guy," Nadia pressed.

"He was…" Charlie inhaled sharply, then just as abruptly released her breath. Blake was impossible to describe. But one fact hovered over the last eight years, and it escaped unbidden from her lips. "Actually, we never dated."

Nadia's eyes narrowed. "Not fair. You're always harping on us not to lie."

Charlie held up one hand in surrender. "I'm telling the truth. We were never officially together." She'd always thought they would be one day—and supposedly

Blake had, too—but their visions for that had clearly been very different.

Blake had been a friend. Her *best* friend for all her high school years and into college. But he'd been so much more than that. He'd cheered at her high school graduation when she crossed the stage with a 4.0. He'd threatened to exact revenge on the guy who stood her up for her first date—she couldn't even remember his name now. And he'd never once looked at her like she was less than because of being a foster kid.

Until he'd stopped looking at her altogether and left without saying goodbye.

Charlie shook off the memories before they could pull her completely under and busied herself tucking the cardboard side flaps inside the box. It'd been so long ago… She had to keep remembering that just because she hadn't found the right guy yet didn't mean the right guy was Blake.

Even if they had been voted by their class "most likely to end up together."

"We never had our timing down, is all. No worries. It's all water under the bridge. Besides, he was allergic to dogs."

"Talk about a deal breaker." Nadia tossed the used spatula into the dishwasher and shut the door.

"Yeah, that's sad." Tori threw the remaining dog cookie in the trash. "Dogs are the best. Especially Waffles."

"I still can't believe you named that poor creature at the shelter Waffles." Nadia leaned against the dishwasher and pointed at Tori. "Doesn't he have enough obstacles in his life?"

"That's what Ms. Rachel gets for letting me pick a name." Tori grinned. "Besides, it fits him. He's blondish-brown and has a bunch of dimples in his skin—like a waffle. I just wish I could keep him with me at Tulip House. We'd have a lot of fun playing hide-and-seek there."

"You and those games."

"He's really good. I never win." Tori laughed.

Nadia peered over at Charlie. "Did Mama Gretchen ever let you have a dog?"

"Nope. That's why I loved going to the animal shelter when I wasn't too much older than you guys." Charlie brushed some crumbs off the counter into her palm, then moved to dust them over the sink. "I never could have a pet until I got my own place."

Nadia scooted out of her way as Charlie moved back to the finished cookies. "Must be nice to be independent."

"It has its pros and cons." Charlie stacked the two full boxes on top of each other. "I need to set this last batch up for sale at the college coffee shop. We can swing by now and drop these off if you guys want to help me."

"Yeah!" Tori beamed.

"Sure. I guess." Nadia's feigned disinterest didn't hide the spark in her eye. She loved going on campus, which was precisely why Charlie had invited her to shadow today. Nadia was bright, and if Charlie could keep her interested and out of trouble—and away from the urge to grow up *too* fast—maybe Nadia could get a scholarship to take community college classes just like Charlie had.

As for Tori, so far, the younger teen seemed less hardened, more pliable. Charlie hoped to make an impact as her CASA before the window of opportunity closed. These girls needed all the advocacy they could get.

Charlie locked up the kitchen and followed both girls to her mini-SUV, hiding a grin as she listened to them squabble over who got to ride shotgun. Maybe Charlie hadn't ever found a true home with Blake like she'd expected. But she'd found it at Tulip House, in her volunteer work at the shelter and in her growing business. And that was enough.

She was content.

Could he ever be content in such a small town?

Blake Bryant thanked the college-aged barista as she handed him his coffee—black—and took the steaming cup to a table by the window overlooking Peach Street. December in Tulip Mound, Kansas, looked much the same after almost a decade away. Well, eight years, to be exact, but who was counting?

The carefully tended tulip patches that normally filled the sidewalks in the spring and summer months now gave way to rich poinsettias, nestled under twinkle lights that glowed year-round. The old-fashioned general store across the street from the community college boasted a familiar, faded red-and-white-striped awning—soon to be dusted in snow if his memory served correctly—and the college campus still seemed to be the only place to get a decent cup of coffee.

For now, anyway.

Blake leaned back against the rickety wooden chair that scraped against the tired tiled floor, noting that, too, hadn't changed, and checked his watch. He had about fifteen minutes to kill until his appointment at the animal shelter.

It'd take more than a few sips of coffee to propel him through the phone appointment he had after that one—talking with a caseworker about his newly discovered niece. But he couldn't let himself dwell on that right now or he'd never make it through his upcoming presentation.

Just thinking about his niece being orphaned for years and him not even realizing it until a week ago… Well, the fact knotted his throat and clenched his stomach.

Helping her was absolutely his top priority, but he had to go about it in a certain order. And first, he had to scope out the new location for his company, Jitter Mugs. Navigating this specific deal should be a breeze—and he desperately needed it to be so. Hopefully it'd be as simple as "sign here, initial here" and then he could get his boss off his back. With last week's life-changing phone call, he needed job security more than ever before—and his boss had made it clear if he flubbed this deal, there'd be major consequences.

The stakes were too high now to fail. His savings wouldn't last long or be that impressive on paper if he got fired at the same time he was trying to potentially start an adoption process.

He took a sip of the steaming brew he'd ordered and licked his lips. Not bad. He was sure even after Jitter Mugs opened, the college café would keep its loyal customers and survive. After all, the students would still need their caffeine jolts to be within easy reach. Jitter Mugs would just be an alternative, with trendier drinks, bringing a taste of the big city to Tulip Mound.

And from the looks of things, Tulip Mound could stand an update. Being back here now for the first time in years made him wonder how he'd ever stayed as long as he had.

Well, there had been *one* motivation for staying…

Flashbacks of a particular five-six, brown-eyed motivation fluttered through his head, bringing memories of blankets at bonfires, endless hours on the phone and shared earbuds for customized playlists. He quickly blinked the images away before they could land. That was a lifetime ago. Blake Meyer didn't exist anymore—literally, according to the state of Kansas.

Besides, with all her personal aspirations…the ones he apparently wasn't worth competing with…there was no way Charlie still lived in—

The bell on the door jingled, interrupting the strains of a jazzy Christmas carol playing over the speakers, and a dark-haired teenager stepped through the frame. She turned to hold it open for a younger teen and a petite woman carrying two large bakery boxes. Long red hair cascaded down the woman's back and over the sleeves of her yellow sweatshirt, reminding him of Charlie. He looked away and took another gulp of coffee. It needed hazelnut.

Then the stranger laughed and turned, and their gazes collided.

Bitter liquid sputtered from his lips. Not just a cute redhead—*his* redhead. Correction, she wasn't his—she'd never been, despite his last-ditch attempt to make it so. His stomach coiled. There she was, his Ghost of Christmas Past, standing ten feet away for the first time in almost a decade.

She hadn't been drinking anything, but he was certain that if she had, she'd be wearing it, too, judging by the way her jaw suddenly unhinged. He fumbled for a napkin, then realized he'd never actually grabbed one in the first place and settled for dragging the back of his hand across the two-day stubble on his chin. He should have shaved. He shouldn't have come.

He should have prepared to face her.

She set the box on the counter, shared a few words with the college student working behind the bar and then took a hesitant step toward him. He meant to get up and take a step toward her in return. Be a gentleman. He'd always had manners—making a new life in Denver eight years ago hadn't changed that. But he somehow seemed permanently attached to the uncomfortable chair beneath him.

The teens who had come in with Charlie lingered at the register, so she approached him alone, her eyes wary, like she'd seen a ghost. In some ways, he probably was.

"Blake?"

He ran a hand over his hair, cut a little shorter than it'd been in his college days. "Hey." Just like everything else in Tulip Mound, she hadn't changed at all. Well, there were more laugh lines in her cheeks, maybe, and her narrow frame had filled out a little, giving her the softer, rounder look of a confident woman. But her eyes—they were the exact same. Wise. Calculating.

Measuring…him?

He would surely still fall short if that was the case.

He took a fortifying breath and stood. He'd secured top dollars with CEOs, led seminars in front of hundreds and talked even the most begrudging shop owners into deals. Maybe he wasn't the cutthroat shark his boss wanted him to be, but he could handle an ex—who really wasn't even an ex on a technicality. What *did* you call someone who once held your heart but never a label?

He politely held out his hand. "It's good to see you, Charlie."

She looked at it, then him, and raised her eyebrows.

Who was he kidding? He should have known the formal approach wouldn't work. Charlie was too…real. He shoved his hands in his pockets, trying to appear casual and hide the incessant pounding of his heart. "You look good." *Understatement, understatement, understatement.*

She still didn't respond, just squinted at him, as if completely unaffected by his opinion. He didn't blame her. But then again, at the end of the day, *she'd* rejected *him.* He had to remember that and not get swept up in the wild waves of her hair or the dimple in her cheek that kept her looking more like the twenty-one-year-old he'd left behind than the…how old was she now? Twenty-nine? One year his junior. But always so far ahead of him in maturity and drive.

At least, that used to be the case. He wasn't the same guy anymore.

Why was it suddenly so important that Charlie know that?

"Thank you." She let out a slow breath, then squared her shoulders, her eyes softening just a little. Maybe she'd had time to absorb the shock. "It's been a long time."

He nodded. "I'm just here on business."

The softening calloused over. "Of course. I wouldn't expect you to stay."

He hadn't meant to sound so defensive. Charlie—and that dimple—put his guard up. He tried again. "Where are you working?"

"I own a pop-up bakery." Her chin lifted slightly.

"So, you did it, then." He wasn't surprised and hated that his tone indicated he was. "I mean, that's great. Congratulations." Now that sounded condescending. He cleared his throat. He'd never been good at off-the-cuff. He needed time to get his thoughts together before making a deal or a presentation. He hated surprises—it was his weakness.

Or maybe Charlie was just his weakness.

She crossed her arms over her yellow shirt. Still guarded. The upbeat instrumental rendition of "Rockin'

Around the Christmas Tree" streaming through the speakers felt out of place with the tension pulsing between them. "What about you?"

He rocked back on his heels, wondering if she really cared or just felt trapped into making small talk. At least this he could answer with confidence. "I'm in expansion and acquisitions for a major coffee chain. They're based in Colorado. Basically, I make deals for new developments."

"Huh."

It wasn't so much a question as a judgment. He stiffened. So, he still wasn't enough for her.

Not that he'd been trying to be.

She continued, "And you said you're in town for work?"

He nodded.

"Right before the holidays?"

He shrugged. "That's business." No one else had wanted to travel so far at the holidays—but for him, it'd been the perfect opportunity. It wasn't like he had a family to spend the holidays with in Colorado anyway— though maybe after this Christmas, he would.

Her eyes narrowed. "Where exactly are you—"

Then the girls who had accompanied her strolled up, their eyes mildly curious as they glanced between the two of them. "Luke said he'd get the treats displayed as usual and keep you posted on any leftovers," the taller, dark-haired one said. "He wants to talk to you later about more Christmas-themed desserts for your next batch."

The younger one rolled her eyes with a little grin. "And yes, before you ask, we made sure to clarify which snacks were for humans and which were for dogs."

"Thanks, girls. You're both a big help." Charlie's brittle expression completely disintegrated when she looked at the teens. It morphed into something sweet…so loving it sort of made Blake wish she'd look at him like that. She had, once upon a time.

But her shield snapped right back into place when she returned her gaze to his. "This is Blake, an old friend of mine." She pointed at him, like he wasn't a whole lot more than a pesky fly she had to deal with.

"I'm Nadia." The dark-haired girl pitched up on the toes of her fuzzy boots, scrutinizing him. "Old friend, huh?" Then her eyes widened, and she pointed. "Wait. You mean like *friend* friend—"

"I'm sorry, we really need to go." Charlie pinched Nadia's sweater sleeve and tugged. "We've got to get to our next bakery drop. It was…uh, good…seeing you." She barely glanced at Blake as she attempted to literally drag both girls toward the door.

"Bye!" The younger one, in a slightly crooked winter hat, turned to wave as they were propelled away.

"Nice to meet you both!" he called after them. Nadia still gaped at him over her shoulder, as if she knew something he didn't. But he *did* know—and he couldn't help but grin like an idiot as he gathered his lackluster coffee and briefcase.

Charlie had been talking about him.

Chapter Two

Charlie hated how long it took for dogs to get adopted in the area. And she hated that most abandoned animals who checked in to the Paradise Paws shelter arrived weary, matted and malnourished.

But right now, she *really* hated the way her hands shook as she shoved them in the back pockets of her jeans. She tried to tell herself it was low blood sugar—she'd been too busy to eat lunch—but deep down, she knew it wasn't a lack of carbs.

More like an overabundance of the past.

Tori grinned as she squatted beside a fluffy mutt in the sprawling, leaf-strewn yard of Paradise Paws. As always, Waffles wasn't far from Tori, crouching beside her and a little white dog. Best Charlie and Rachel had been able to tell, Waffles was mostly basset hound, due to his droopy folds of skin and trademark long ears, but he was taller than expected—possibly mixed with a shepherd of some kind.

And currently very jealous of the attention Tori doled out to the other dog. He barked, and she immediately switched to petting both animals—one with each hand. "Isn't this guy adorable? Pompoms are so funny looking."

"It's *Pomeranian*," Nadia corrected. She stood with arms crossed and attempted to look indifferent as a black terrier mix yapped up at her. "Not pompom."

The two girls had passed out the peanut butter Santa hat minicakes to multiple drooling, eager mouths. Then they'd hung around to play fetch while Charlie waited on her friend Rachel to come out of her office—unfortunately leaving Charlie plenty of time to replay the events with Blake at the coffee shop in her mind on repeat.

"Pom is a nickname." Tori averted her eyes she stroked the dog's back. "Like mine. Tori instead of Victoria."

Charlie's heart simultaneously wrung and swelled. Swelled with the joy of being able to provide the connection at Paradise Paws for Tori that she so desperately needed—and wrung with the fact that the sweet girl needed it at all.

Nadia opened her mouth with a retort, then must have caught the glare Charlie sent in her direction, because she instantly snapped her mouth shut and had the decency to look chagrined. She tossed her scarf over her shoulder and bent down to pet Waffles. "Whatever you say—Tor."

"*Tori*," the younger girl corrected. Then her hands froze midstroke over the Pomeranian's back, and she snorted a laugh. "Never mind, I see what you did."

"There you go." Nadia leaned over and slapped her a high five. "Stick with me, kid."

Charlie shook her head as she leaned against the exterior brick wall of the shelter and tilted her face to the winter afternoon sun, letting it thaw the chill that had taken up residence inside. If that entire exchange between the girls just now wasn't confirmation that Charlie had zero time to spare thinking about Blake, she didn't know what was. The teens—and the others at Tulip House— needed her. Her time was well spent giving back, not fretting over unrequited love from the past. She'd moved on years ago. Who cared if Blake was in town?

And yet there he was anyway, creeping back into her thoughts just as stealthily as he'd appeared in the coffee shop. All these years, and he just showed back up—and for work, no less. Like there weren't plenty of clients for him to do whatever he'd alluded to doing in Colorado. What had he said…deals for new development? He sounded just like the everyday villain in a suit that everyone in those made-for-TV movies tried to avoid.

A golden retriever mix leaned against Charlie's leg, coating her jeans with fur as he panted. She bent down and rubbed his head, happy for the distraction. He was sweet, just like her own adopted schnauzer, Cooper. Strange how some of the dogs needed all the affection you could give them, while other dogs watched warily and preferred you keep your physical distance. Charlie's gaze landed on Nadia and Tori.

Maybe not that strange after all.

The outside screen door slammed shut, and she stood as the shelter manager, Rachel Rose, approached.

Rachel smiled warmly, but it didn't quite seem to counter the stress lines creasing her olive cheeks. "Thanks for bringing the dog treats—and the extra volunteers." She nodded toward the girls, who had donned bright-colored gloves and moved on to playing tug-of-war with the Pomeranian. "We can use as many hands as we can get these days."

"Of course. You know we love it here." Then Charlie paused, reading between the lines, and her heart sank.

She knelt to adjust the buffalo-plaid bandanna tied around the golden's neck. "That bad, huh?"

Rachel tucked a strand of dark hair behind her ear as she surveyed the two-acre property. The grounds were beautiful, with lush hills and wildflowers in the spring and inviting piles of snow in the winter, perfect for sledding. It all backed up to a pond where several of the water-loving dogs frequently splashed—when it wasn't frozen over. "Donations have been down for a while, and we didn't get the boost we usually do at this point in the year. Plus, you remember, Widow Peterson passed away last summer, and her annual donation was always substantial." She hesitated. "There's an interested party, though."

"Interested in what?" Charlie straightened, and the retriever ran to Tori, knocking her beanie off her head and tugging her ponytail in his teeth. Then Waffles joined in, jumping on Tori's lap. The girl burst out laughing. Charlie couldn't help but smile back. This shelter had been a lifesaver for the teens in so many ways. Not only had volunteering taught them responsibility, but it'd also given them another source of the love and affection most of the girls were sorely lacking. That connection was so important to Tori—to them all.

Rachel picked at the sleeve of her purple T-shirt, avoiding Charlie's gaze. "I'm not quite sure the angle yet. But there's a man who called and asked to come to see the property." She shrugged, like it wasn't crucial.

But something cold and entirely unwelcome washed over her, and it had nothing to do with the Kansas December temps. "So, like maybe a potential investor in the nonprofit?"

Rachel sighed as she bent down to scoop up Buster,

a little black-and-brown mutt. "Maybe." Her tone indicated she knew more than she was letting on, but she couldn't—wouldn't?—elaborate further. "It's hard to say yet. They were very vague on the phone. Just requested an in-person meeting."

"Is Paradise Paws in danger?" Stress knotted in Charlie's chest. They couldn't shut down the only no-kill shelter in the vicinity. There was nothing else like it in Tulip Mound—or anywhere nearby in Kansas. What would happen to all the dogs? Where would people bring strays or unwanted pets?

The answer loomed, obvious—the pound.

"All I can say is that our bottom line is more red than black lately. And our contract for renting the property here from Mr. Raines is coming to an end next month after the New Year." Rachel's lips pursed, and she opened her mouth, then shut it. She didn't have to finish her sentence to answer Charlie's question.

Was Paradise Paws in danger? *Yes.*

Charlie's stomach twisted, and she reached over to take Buster from Rachel. She needed a hug from the little guy. "Maybe the man you're meeting will save the day." That happened, right? It did in books and movies, anyway. Surely it could happen for such a good cause as the shelter.

"Anything's possible. And I've been praying," Rachel conceded and scooped up another canine that trotted past, as if she, too, needed the furry comfort. She rested her chin against the scraggly pup's head and finally met Charlie's gaze dead-on. "But my gut tells me it's not going to be simple."

Charlie pressed her lips together as she set the black-and-brown mutt back on the ground. He scampered over to Nadia, who looked around surreptitiously before pick-

ing him up and rubbing his lopsided ears. Tori witnessed
the exchange and crept closer to Nadia, reaching up to rub
the dog's head. Briefly, her cheek rested against Nadia's
shoulder as they cooed over the furry animal, and for
once, the older teen didn't push away the younger one's
constant need for affection. They stood huddled around
the puppy together while Waffles jumped up on Tori's
leg, demanding attention.

Charlie's heart pounded an erratic rhythm. This
couldn't happen. Whoever this man was, whatever the
deal was, she'd make sure it came out for the best.

The screen door creaked behind them. "Excuse me for
letting myself in. No one answered at the front." A sneeze
followed the deep baritone filling the late-afternoon air.

Charlie turned at the same time as Rachel. "Blake?"

Zero contact in eight years, yet here they were, face-
to-face twice in one day. If he had been determined to
abandon their friendship, then thankfully, he'd moved
away and essentially vanished years ago. Her heart
couldn't have taken this kind of daily running into each
other. She squeezed her shaking hands into fists.

"Charlie." He blinked rapidly, eyes watering, and
pressed a handkerchief to his reddened nose. Confusion
flickered across his face. Then he glanced between her
and Rachel, easing slightly away when his gaze rested
on the dog in Rachel's arms. "I didn't realize you were
in another meeting. Ms. Rose, I presume?"

"That's me." Rachel set the dog down, then held out
her hand to shake his. "And no worries. You're right on
time for our appointment."

Charlie frowned. *Appointment?*

Her friend gestured toward the door. "Right this way.

We can talk in my office." She shot Charlie a wide-eyed glance as she gestured for Blake to go in front of her.

He hesitated, his eyes lingering on Charlie's, then sneezed into his elbow as he stepped inside. "My apologies. I'm allergic to dogs."

Charlie scoffed. Then recognition hit, as hard as the allergies currently attacking Blake. *I make deals for new developments.*

Indignation rose in her throat, and her jaw clenched. Blake was most definitely *not* going to be saving the day.

Ms. Rose's office was stuffy and covered in dog hair, warm from the space heater blowing beside her desk. Blake brushed at the faux-leather chair to rid it of tiny white hairs before he sat on the edge and fought back yet another sneeze. He should have met with the owner at the campus coffee shop instead of coming to the shelter, but he hadn't realized the animals would have free rein of the interior.

Plus, for maximum success, he needed to scope out the acreage for himself before presenting his deal. His boss at Jitter Mugs would be ecstatic if he could negotiate an arrangement under their top offer—which would only make Blake look better.

And if his life was going to change as significantly as he imagined it was about to, he was going to need all the professional and financial blessings he could get.

One phone call had changed his life and would very likely change a young girl's life as well…possibly providing an amazing Christmas present for them both.

It was a lot for a Friday afternoon.

Blake cleared his throat, then set his briefcase on the carpet beside the chair, making a mental note to wipe the fur off later. "Ms. Rose, as I'm sure you're aware, Jitter Mugs is prepared to offer a favorable price for your property." He tried to look professional, despite the fact he must resemble Rudolph the Red-Nosed Reindeer from his allergies and the winter wind. Not exactly the lasting impression he wanted to leave on a potential seller— or Charlie.

He leaned forward and attempted to shove thoughts of her away, but they lingered, sticky. Sort of like the dog hair on his loafers.

"Please, call me Rachel." She reached over to straighten the crooked limb on the tiny desktop Christmas tree. "I'm actually not familiar with why you're here. I was assuming you'd be able to shed more light on why you made this appointment?"

"Of course." Blake struggled to keep his face an impassive mask as irritation churned. Not again. His new admin assistant back at their home office in Denver was growing notorious for not getting details straight. She was supposed to have done this grunt work for him, paving the way for him to swoop in with his offer. Now he and his company looked disorganized. Definitely not how he wanted to come across to Charlie.

No. He meant the *seller*. Not how he wanted to come across to the *seller*. He scrubbed his hand over his chin. He needed to focus.

Except...

He frowned and stood abruptly. "Excuse me."

Rachel's eyes widened as he gave her a brief nod, then strode swiftly to the office door she'd shut behind them. He wrenched it open, and, just as he expected, Charlie tumbled into the room, nearly knocking over the fake potted fern beside the door.

Her face blossomed as red as her hair.

He let out a slow sigh as he studied her. "Perhaps a water glass would have helped you hear more clearly."

Charlie straightened with a surprising amount of dignity for someone in her position and lifted her chin. "I wasn't eavesdropping. I was just—"

"Listening uninvited through a closed door?" Blake crossed his arms over his chest, partly to curb his annoyance and partly to suppress the urge to sweep her into a giant "I miss you" hug. He hadn't seen her face that particular shade of cherry since the night he— Well. Since that November night when he'd professed his long-budding feelings and then left her standing alone in the twilight.

Charlie plopped—still uninvited—into the faux-leather chair set beside his. "I know why you're here, and I wanted to stop you before this went any further."

"How could you possibly know why I'm here?" Blake refused to sit, refused to acknowledge she had any business even being in the room. In running through all the various scenarios of returning to his hometown, this one hadn't made the list.

But she wasn't deterred. Neither did she seem affected by the slight crease in Rachel's forehead and the way the woman opened her mouth, then shut it and lifted one shoulder. Apparently, Charlie was still Charlie, and everyone had accepted that.

She just hadn't accepted *him*.

Fine. She might know why he was there, as in, there at Paradise Paws today. But she didn't know—*couldn't* know, and as far as he was concerned, *wouldn't* know— why he had come home in the first place. Why he'd agreed to negotiate this deal that, a week ago, he'd have run far away from.

He might not have been to church in a hot minute, but he recognized a providential sign when he saw one.

"I'm really not following." Rachel's tone, low and carefully drawn out, broke through his and Charlie's silent stare down. "Can someone please explain what's going on?"

"Happy to. This guy—" Charlie jerked her head toward him, her eyes accusing "—is here to shut down the shelter."

"No, I'm not." Blake shook his head as he reluctantly sat in the chair next to the glaring redhead. "If I could speak for myself…" He shot Charlie a pointed look before turning back to Rachel.

"Oh…" The shelter manager's gaze darted between the two of them, then her eyes lit. *"Ohh."*

"No way." Charlie waved her hand erratically at Rachel. The long sleeve of her yellow sweatshirt bunched up on her forearm. "It's not what you're thinking."

Now he was the one confused. He glanced back and forth, from Rachel's smirk to Charlie's wide-eyed denial. "Ladies?"

Rachel's grin resembled a plump cat who had *no* idea where the missing canary had gone. "Right." Her dark eyes danced at Charlie. "Of course not."

"Can you please focus on the fact that this man is trying to shut down Paradise Paws? At *Christmas*?" Charlie's ire returned—this time directed back at Blake.

He fought the urge to scoot farther away in his seat. "I'm *not* shutting down the shelter." He held up both hands. "I'm here to work out a deal. There's a very generous offer on the table, one that, in my opinion, Paradise Paws would be wise to take."

"That's just it." Charlie twisted in her seat to face him. "No one asked for your opinion."

The battle to stay professional raged against the battle to tell Charlie exactly what he was thinking. But that was still dangerous, because his thoughts volleyed back and forth between telling her off for her brazenness… and letting her know exactly how beautiful she'd become over the last several years.

"I think that's up to Ms. Rose to decide." He corralled his thoughts back to business. The sooner he landed this deal, the sooner he could switch gears and further pursue the real reason he was here.

To get to know his niece.

Chapter Three

"Me?" Rachel pressed a finger against her purple top. "I don't follow."

Charlie shifted to catch Blake's reaction. He obviously was missing a big piece of this puzzle laid out before him.

Calm and professional—a stark contrast to the indignation ready to boil over in her own heart—he leaned back in his chair and crossed one ankle over the other. "Naturally, you. You're the owner." Blake gestured around the small office with one hand. A diffuser releasing cinnamon-scented bursts from the corner of Rachel's desk gurgled in response.

"I'm the *manager* of the nonprofit," Rachel corrected. She leaned back, her desk chair squeaking. "Paradise Paws doesn't own the property. Neither do I. We rent this space and the acreage for the dogs."

A shadow skidded across Blake's face. Eight years, and Charlie could still read him like her favorite baking magazine. He hadn't known that key detail before coming in the room, and he was going to do everything he could to play it off now. Because that had always been Blake—hide every emotion, hide anything that could make a situation awkward…like every time she'd ever asked him about his family. He'd joke about his dad being a candidate for any good reality TV show and change the subject. Or that time at the Sweet Briar Café when she'd inquired about how close he and his older sister were, and he'd simply answered with a vague "not very" and proceeded to fold his napkin into an origami swan.

This should be entertaining. What distraction method would he go for this time? She crossed her arms over her sweatshirt and waited.

But the shadow in Blake's expression dissolved. He spread his hands—one still clutching a tissue—wide across his lap in submission. "I'm sorry for the confusion."

Charlie blinked. Blake, apologizing? She frowned, unsure if she should grab on to something solid, because surely the earth was tilting on its axis.

He kept going. "I thought I was here to present a deal to the landowner on behalf of my company. My sources told me that was you."

"I understand. And I wish I had the authority to accept—*or* reject." Rachel's emphasis was all the subtext they should have needed. But Blake had never been one to pick up on hints.

Charlie slid to the edge of her chair, her heart pounding a hard rhythm in her chest. It wasn't because of Blake's proximity. Or the way his shorter haircut really made his jawline more rugged or the five o'clock shadow that completely suited him. No, her out-of-control pulse was one hundred percent because he was not here to save the day—he was here to ruin it. Always Blake with the selfish intentions, looking out for number one and not worrying about whom he hurt. Did he not care that a dozen animals could get sent to their doom if he proceeded as planned?

"Why this particular property?" Charlie asked. "Couldn't your coffee shop go somewhere else?"

"Jitter Mugs locations have a unique brand." Blake drummed his fingers on his knee. "They like to acquire properties on acreage with venue potential, to expand their audience for additional revenue." He shrugged. "You won't see one on a busy corner in Chicago or Dallas. You'll see most of them on the outskirts of the city, or in quaint small towns." He gestured around them to punctuate his point. "Hence, Tulip Mound. The acreage and pond are ideal for their brand."

Charlie looked at Rachel, whose neutral expression remained in place, even though she knew she and her friend were thinking the same thing—*find somewhere else.*

"I'm sorry to have wasted your time." Blake reached for his briefcase and stood. "I'll just be heading out before I keep sneezing all over your furniture here." He let out a half-hearted chuckle. Rachel smiled politely.

But Charlie wasn't done. "Wait. You don't understand." Without thinking, she reached out and grabbed his arm. His surprisingly muscular, corded arm, even under a lightweight blazer. She snatched her hand back. When was the last time she'd touched him?

That night after Thanksgiving eight years ago. When he'd wrapped her in a hug big enough to take her breath away and then walked off, leaving her arms aching for more and her heart breaking into a thousand pieces on the grass at her feet.

Blake arched his brow as he stood over her. "I don't understand what?"

She shook her head to clear it. He wasn't joining her on memory lane. He was all business, staring at her like a near stranger. Like a disinterested acquaintance, who was swooping in to take everything she'd invested in and loved away from her.

Again.

She stood to face him, eager to level the playing field, and tried to keep the past in the past and focus on this present emergency. Maybe Blake tended to avoid conflict, but she was willing to face it to protect the ones she loved.

She'd have done that for him years ago if he'd just let her.

She took a steadying breath. "Paradise Paws rents this land. If you work a deal to sell, the shelter will have to move."

Blake shrugged and shifted his briefcase to his other hand. "I'm not seeing the issue. Nonprofits change locations all the time. I'm sure there are several suitable places all over Tulip Mound to carry on business as usual." He checked his watch.

"You still don't get it." Charlie inhaled sharply and then released her breath in a huff—hopefully one loud enough to hide the tears threatening her voice. She glanced at Rachel, whose slow nod confirmed Charlie's worst fear.

"Get what, Ms. Bussey?" An edge of impatience coated his tone.

"Paradise Paws is already struggling to survive—financially." She squared off with his arresting gaze, ignoring his attempt to keep her at arm's length with the use of her formal name. "If we lose this favorable rent arrangement, there's nowhere else for us to go."

Well, that hadn't gone as planned.

Blake stood by his rental car, fumbling with his keys. He'd already done enough damage in this brief stint back home, and he hadn't even met his niece yet. But he couldn't let down his boss—or his future. There was still the giant question mark dangling over it all, and no time for things to get derailed. He had to make this deal. And apparently, now he had to do his own grunt work and look up the contact info for the real landowner himself. Clearly, asking Rachel for that information after Charlie's outburst would be a faux pas. He just needed to regroup and start over with his original plan.

Which would probably have to wait until Monday, seeing how Friday's business hours were officially over. He wasn't about to cold-call a potential seller on a weekend.

He bit back a groan as he tossed his briefcase onto the passenger seat of the luxury sedan. This deal should have been so simple. Instead, he'd approached the wrong person, looked incompetent—at best—and, to make matters worse, he'd had no idea the shelter wouldn't have a place to move to if the deal was accepted.

He'd never worried about the aftermath of his negotiations before. His boss had trained him not to. "Get in, get the deal and get out" was the company's unofficial motto. It wasn't any of their business what happened in the wake of their buyouts, a fact that hadn't sat well with Blake when he first started the job, and even less so this last year as his priorities began to shift. What they did often left a lot of loose ends, and while legally it might not be their concern, morally, it bothered him.

And now, he looked like a jerk who wanted to make a bunch of dogs homeless.

At Christmas.

A door slammed. Blake looked up just in time to see Charlie barreling down the front steps of the shelter, aiming straight for him. He braced himself, legs apart, even though all his instincts shouted for him to get in the car and drive away.

Her voice flamed as bright as her hair. If there'd been snow on the ground yet this season, it'd have melted in her wake. "A word, *Mr. Meyer*?"

Ouch. Though he probably deserved that. He crossed his arms. "It's actually Mr. Bryant now." He hadn't wanted to point that out this early in his visit—or at all—but as usual, Charlie left him no choice.

Her fire extinguished slightly, and she hesitated a few steps away from him. "You changed your last name? To your middle name?"

He nodded, offering no explanation—there wasn't one he was willing to give right now. And, to be honest, he couldn't trust her with the information. Not with so much ammo loaded in her eyes.

She planted her hands on her hips and let out a slow breath. "Look, I don't know why you're here, or what's going on. Or why you changed your name." Her brows furrowed, and she licked her lips.

He forced himself to look away, lest his thoughts go racing back down sunlit paths better left unexplored.

"But I need you to reconsider this."

Oh, brother. He opened his car door, putting it neatly between them. The more layers separating them, the better. "I'm sorry the shelter is struggling, I really am. But I'm sure something will work out." He sniffed, his nose finally starting to recover from the onslaught of animal dander.

She shaded her eyes with one hand and squinted up at him against the late-afternoon sun, which shot golden highlights into her red hair. Good grief, she'd gotten even more beautiful than when he'd left.

"There is one solution." Her voice trailed off.

"Great. Go with that, then." He couldn't make Charlie's problems his own. She'd rejected him and a true partnership years ago. He owed her nothing—and he had so much on his proverbial plate right now that adding one more item could tip the whole thing over.

Now to escape. He slid onto the driver's seat and put on his sunglasses.

Charlie moved to prevent him from shutting the door. "The solution is don't do it. Don't give Mr.—don't give the owner the option to kick us out."

She'd almost slipped and given him a head start toward what he needed. But the facts remained. "Charlie, that's not a solution." He pressed two fingers against his throbbing temple. She'd always been somewhat stubborn, but this adult version of Charlie had matured into a full-on bulldog. "I *have* to. It's my job." She didn't know the rest, didn't know the why. And couldn't.

She leaned one jeans-clad hip against his open car door. "So, we're back to Charlie now? Not *Ms. Bussey?*"

He looked up, daring to meet her gaze. "I was trying to establish some professionalism. It wasn't meant to be a slam."

"You used to give me the T-shirts you outgrew, Blake. I think we're past professionalism." Hurt danced in her eyes, mirroring the same emotion currently thudding a protest in his heart.

He opened his mouth, unsure what to say—and terrified that his real thoughts on how cute she used to be in those faded tees would come slipping out instead.

A dog barked, saving him from having to respond. Several female shouts rang across the yard. Then the two teens from the college campus, now both wearing beanies and scarves, opened the wooden gate on the side of the property and came spilling out, laughing as they attempted to corral the dogs back inside the secured yard.

Nadia, the taller girl, swung her dark braid over her shoulder as she wrestled the lock into place, while the shorter teen approached Charlie. A bright smile coated her face, her cheeks flushed from the cold. "Guess what? We finally taught Henrietta how to roll over."

"Awesome job, Tori!" Charlie slapped her a high five as she drew closer. "I knew you could do it."

He gripped the steering wheel with both hands, his palms suddenly slick. His heartbeat accelerated, and he cleared his throat. He hadn't caught her name earlier in the coffee shop with the other teen, so he hadn't made the connection. But here she was, once again, standing before him in real time.

Tori Sutton.

His niece.

Chapter Four

"Then he turned pale, shut the door and drove away. Just like that." Charlie wiped dust off a snow globe from Gretchen's collection with a cloth rag, careful not to take her frustration out on the delicate glass hosting a group of singing carolers. It wasn't the first time in her life that Blake had walked away from her while she'd been upset, and at this rate, she wondered if it'd be the last.

"Maybe you shouldn't have brought up wearing his old T-shirts." Gretchen Jolie was short, slender and had long dark hair streaked with strands of gray that she usually wore in a no-nonsense low ponytail. Her eyes, bright and full of wisdom, shone with understanding and more than a little amusement as she handed Charlie another globe from the cardboard box—this one showcasing an ice-skating rink inside.

"I'm sure you're right. But he was talking to me so formally—I couldn't help but put him in his place."

Gretchen smiled as she pulled several more globes free from their yearlong storage. "Men don't usually like that."

"Especially prideful ones." After everything they'd been through together, Charlie still couldn't believe he'd called her Ms. Bussey. It'd hurt more than it should. But maybe she'd just been overly sensitive from the shock of realizing his purpose in coming to Paradise Paws.

Gretchen stuffed the cardboard flaps back into the empty box. "You believe Blake is prideful now? Has he changed that much over the years?"

"You should have seen him, all stuffy and buttoned-up, acting like he barely knew me. He was all business." And carefully corralled muscle. But that wasn't the point.

Charlie set the clean globes on the coffee table, then arched her back in a stretch from her slumped position. She'd been sitting on the floor in the Jolies' living room for the past half hour, venting in hushed tones while she helped Gretchen set out her traditional display. It wasn't Christmas at the Jolie house if every square inch of the living room didn't hold a snow globe of some size. It'd been one of her favorite traditions at Tulip House over the years. Hopefully the teen residents would draw the same comfort from them that she had.

And maybe that was what hurt the most. Blake had left her years ago, even knowing her history, knowing that everyone else in her life had left at some point…and then to stroll back into Tulip Mound like he'd barely even known her was the last heartless straw.

Gretchen scooted the cardboard box out of the way and stood. "Is professional all that bad? Blake was always a smart boy. I'm glad to hear he's become successful."

Sweet Gretchen. Always looking for the best in people. Unfortunately, she had Blake all wrong. "Successful maybe, but not at the right thing. He only came home to take away something I love." Charlie shook her head, refusing to let the emotion threatening the back of her throat free. She reached for her phone to check her texts as a distraction, but her pockets were empty. She'd probably left it in her car.

"And what are you going to do about that threat?" Gretchen began arranging snow globes of various sizes on the mantel above the fireplace.

"I don't know yet. But I *can* tell you I'm much more likely to turn into Mrs. Claus than I am to let him get away with it." Steel strengthened Charlie's voice—and her backbone. "He must not remember who he's messing with."

Blake had hurt her once, and she'd already grieved that loss. But she refused to let him mess with those animals—or the teens who loved them. Neither the dogs nor the girls had many people willing to fight for them.

Charlie was more than happy to go down swinging on their behalf.

"It's okay to miss him, you know." Gretchen's voice was quiet but effective. The words slipped over and inside the cracked pieces of Charlie's tired armor.

"Maybe. But I don't miss whoever this new person is." If she thought too long about the boy Blake used to be and what she'd lost, she'd probably let loose the tears still knocking around behind her eyes. And that wouldn't do anyone any good.

The heater cranked on with a hum, giving them a little more white-noise cover. The teens—who this year were Nadia, Sabrina, Riley and now Tori—were supposed to be in bed for quiet time before lights-out, but Charlie knew that wasn't a guarantee…especially if they knew she was still there, having a private conversation with the house mother.

Charlie had brought the girls back to Tulip House after they left Paradise Paws earlier that evening, and Art had convinced her to stay for dinner. At first, she'd resisted, since she needed to get home to Cooper—but the aroma of sizzling steaks had coerced her. With a belly full of loaded baked potatoes and beef, and the promise to herself that she'd bring Cooper home the leftovers, she'd waited around until she had Gretchen alone.

She was the closest thing Charlie had ever had to a mom.

"Holidays can be hard." Gretchen came around the coffee table, extended her hands to Charlie and hauled her to her feet. She pressed her hands on either side of Charlie's face, stared her straight in the eyes and smiled the same patient smile she'd given Charlie years ago when she'd come home from junior year with an F on her second-semester report card. "So, I want you to remember one word."

"Revenge?" Charlie half joked, half hiccupped. The tears were coming, like it or not.

"*No,*" Gretchen scolded with a chuckle. "Emmanuel."

"God with us." Charlie finished the sentiment by heart as she dabbed at her eyes. It was a lesson Art and Gretchen had drilled into her from her first Christmas at their house, when she was almost fifteen, long before it'd been converted into Tulip House. Long before the dream to host multiple teen girls had been conceived in Gretchen's heart and come to fruition.

"You're never alone." Gretchen pulled her into a quick hug. "And remember—sadness and anger are linked. You're usually not feeling one without being too far from the other."

"You're right." Charlie let out a long breath and then a reluctant grin. "As usual."

"I wish you could get those teenagers up there to agree

with you on that." Gretchen winked. "Now, look, I happen to know Art stashed two leftover pieces of brownie from that tin the girls ate their way through after dinner. I'm pretty sure he could be convinced to let you have one of them."

"Sounds good." She squeezed Gretchen's hand before following her into the kitchen. Blake's sudden reappearance at this vulnerable time of year had thrown her off-kilter, that was all. She'd remain grounded in truth—the truth of Emmanuel—and keep a heart of gratitude that God had seen fit to put her in Art's and Gretchen's lives.

Blake couldn't threaten any of her true securities.

"Look who I found!" Art's big dad voice boomed from the foyer off the kitchen just as Gretchen pulled the leftover brownies free from their hiding place in the fridge. He poked his graying head around the door frame. "The prodigal son has returned!"

A figure stepped around the corner, wearing a formal coat and plaid scarf.

Blake.

Holding Charlie's cell phone.

Blake hoped he never had reason to go to court, because the look Charlie pinned him with as she stared across the kitchen had the same effect as slamming a gavel.

He held out the phone like a peace offering, and she crossed the room in three quick strides to snatch it from his hands. "How did you get this?" Fire lit her voice, a reflection of that long red hair she tossed over her shoulder. Once upon a time, he'd had the right to sit close to her, inhale her coconut-scented shampoo and even brush those untamed strands off her face.

Not so much anymore.

"I didn't steal it, if that's what you mean." Riled up by the fact that she was riled up when he was the one doing her a favor, Blake attempted a steadying breath. "You must have dropped it inside my car door when we were… talking…earlier." Talking, arguing, debating—whatever.

Her flame extinguished to a simmer. "Oh. Right." She unlocked her phone and skimmed it, then looked up with a tight nod. "Thank you."

"You're welcome." He shuffled his feet a little, unsure what to say next or how to make a graceful exit. He hadn't wanted to come by this house full of memories in the first place, but he couldn't exactly keep her phone once it'd rolled under his feet while driving back to his B&B after he'd eaten alone at the Sweet Briar Café.

He'd chatted with Tori's caseworker, Anita Duncan, on the phone for twenty minutes while downing a bowl of chicken and dumplings. At his request, she'd given him a few days to get to know Tori before announcing his identity to her or her CASA volunteer. "It'd be best if you met with the CASA volunteer first," Anita had urged. "She'll be able to help you connect with Tori in ways that I'm not as familiar with. That's the beauty of CASA—they're assigned one child at a time, while I'm overseeing multiple."

He'd promised he would take that step eventually—he just needed a few more days to adjust to the whole idea. Now he had to find a way to connect with Tori ASAP. Earlier, when he realized who Tori was and that she must be close to Charlie if she'd been hanging out with her all afternoon, he'd panicked. He didn't know what to say— so many things he *couldn't* say quite yet—and with the lingering argument between them, he'd decided driving away to regroup was his best option.

Until her phone demanded otherwise. How did Charlie manage to interfere with his plans even when she wasn't there?

"It's good to see you, Blake." Gretchen's warm voice filled the awkward spaces lingering in the kitchen. She held out her arms, and before he could decide if it was weird, she pulled him into a hug. As if the past eight years hadn't happened at all.

It didn't appear that Charlie would be offering that much grace.

He hugged Gretchen back, the tension melting from his shoulders. She'd always been a good woman—in fact, she and Art had unofficially taken him in as one of theirs, even as they officially took in foster kids. Charlie had lived with them since she was a freshman in high school, and he'd befriended her when he was a sophomore. He'd spent many afternoons eating cookies in this kitchen—which, judging by the brightly colored floral art on the walls and the faux tulips holding court in a milk jug on the table—hadn't changed much in the past eight years.

And now, Tori was experiencing the same care. It blew his mind.

Art slapped him on the shoulder, as tall, jovial and big-hearted as always. Though what exactly had he meant by the prodigal son comment? "Welcome home, my boy."

"Thank you, sir." Blake shook Art's oversize hand. "But I'm just in town on business." There he went again, defaulting to the same defensive statement he'd given Charlie when he first saw her in the coffee shop that afternoon. Or maybe he kept repeating it because it was the only answer he could supply.

"Would you like a brownie?" Gretchen went back to the kitchen island, where two generously portioned brownies perched atop a candy cane–striped plate. Gretchen had always gone all out for Christmas. Even as his own family had largely ignored the holiday, every time he stepped into the Jolies' residence in high school, it was as if he'd entered a festive wonderland. As a teen, he'd been amused by the abundance of decorations, but now he appreciated it in a fresh way.

In the moment, he hadn't realized what he'd missed. But now, as an adult, he could recognize all that he'd lost growing up.

Charlie shot him a look, and he started to decline, but Gretchen was already placing his brownie on a napkin and sliding it his way. It'd be rude to resist.

Besides, they smelled amazing.

He took the bar stool at the island and tentatively took a bite. An abundance of chocolate burst in his mouth, the chill from the fridge giving the brownies that crispy top shell he'd always liked. "These are amazing, Gretchen. As always."

Charlie bristled as she took the stool next to him—pulling it several inches away first—and claimed the other brownie. "Art made those."

Oops. Yet another strike. Mouth full, he toasted Art with his remaining portion of dessert.

"Just a box mix, but the teens around here don't seem to mind." Art slid a chair out from the table at the breakfast nook beside them while Gretchen turned on the coffeepot.

"You'll have a cup. It's half-caff." Her calm, declarative statement left no room for argument. And surprisingly enough, Blake realized he didn't want to argue. Lingering in a warm kitchen full of Christmas decorations and the scent of fresh coffee, with two out of three people who genuinely seemed happy to see him, was a far more appealing option than returning to his cold B&B room alone.

They chatted aimlessly about the December weather while Gretchen poured steaming mugs of dark roast and placed one before each of them.

Art leaned forward, bracing his forearms on the table as he held his mug between both hands. "What business brings you to town?"

Charlie stiffened beside him as Gretchen glanced at them and then made a not-so-subtle attempt to change the subject. "Art, honey, did you want creamer in your coffee?"

Blake drew a deep breath. Gretchen must know the answer, or she wouldn't have interrupted that way. Charlie had already gotten to her.

"I'm fine, dear." Art blew into his mug. "As I was saying, Blake…sounds like business is good if you're traveling this far for it." He watched Blake over the rim of his cup.

He knew about the shelter, too. He had to. This felt like a test. Blake took a small sip of the still-hot liquid to stall. Definitely needed hazelnut.

"Yeah, Blake, how's business?" Charlie twisted to face him on her stool, a slight challenge in her eyes.

He carefully tugged his professional mask back into place. It'd been nice letting it down for a moment, at least. "It's booming. We're really busy with expansions."

He rattled off a few stats about Jitter Mugs that might mean something to Art, depending on how much the older man kept up with various business magazines. Blake's boss insisted he stay up-to-date on the facts of where their company stood in the daily rise and fall of the industry in case potential sellers needed to be impressed.

But it didn't impress Blake anymore. Neither did his boss's comments of "you need more teeth, Bryant" and "I employ sharks, not guppies."

Gretchen laid a hand on Charlie's shoulder, the same gently restraining motion he'd seen the woman do a hundred times over the years in an effort to curb Charlie's redheaded temper. "It sounds like you've done really well for yourself."

He nodded his thanks. He had. So why did he still feel so empty?

And why the sudden urge to justify his career choices?

He opened his mouth, then thought better of it. He couldn't go into the details of why he needed this deal to go through so badly. Not yet—maybe not ever. He lifted one shoulder in what he hoped was a casual shrug. "I have plans for more." There. That was the truth.

If only they knew how much more.

Chapter Five

Charlie tipped back her mug to finish downing her coffee, the bitter liquid lukewarm at best now. But filling her mouth kept her from blurting out the thoughts racing through her mind, mostly centered around how selfish Blake had become. He was obviously doing well for himself, both strategically and financially, yet he openly admitted to wanting more? He couldn't ever just be content where he was—namely, in Tulip Mound—and worse than that, he didn't even have the decency to try to hide his disdain for her hometown.

Their hometown.

He'd even changed his name. Who was he anymore? And why was he sitting in the Jolies' kitchen like old times? Nothing made sense.

And she had no more coffee to distract her mouth.

Charlie set the empty mug down with a clank. "You know—"

Blake suddenly stood up. He held up one finger, then moved quickly past her to the closed door that separated the kitchen from the formal dining room they typically only utilized at holidays. He pointed to it, then raised his eyebrows at Gretchen.

She checked her watch, then let out an amused sigh. "Honestly, I'm not surprised. Go ahead." She motioned for Blake to continue.

In one fluid motion, he opened the door.

Sabrina, Nadia, Tori and Riley tumbled out on top of each other.

"What *is* that—your superpower?" Charlie asked Blake as the girls scrambled to right themselves in a flurry of fluffy robes, fuzzy house shoes and guilty giggles.

"With you around, I guess they come by the habit honestly." Blake shot Charlie a pointed look, and she couldn't quite decipher if he was annoyed or amused. Maybe both.

Art cleared his throat, and the chaotic commotion stopped. The girls lined up in front of the island, Nadia stroking her braid, Tori still giggling, and Sabrina and Riley—both fifteen as of this past summer—examining their nails as they attempted to hide their smiles.

Art drummed his fingers on the table, his expression stern but his eyes kind. "And why exactly is everyone up eavesdropping instead of in their rooms?"

"We're sorry." Nadia, being the oldest of the four, typically answered any questions first. Her defensive posture didn't exactly match the apologetic words, but she'd come a long way with respect in the past year. Charlie was proud of her.

"We heard voices." Tori gestured toward Blake, who had stepped out of the way and lingered awkwardly on the far side of the island, trapped between the girls and his abandoned bar stool.

"Yeah, *male* voices." Sabrina giggled.

Riley slapped at her arm.

"What? You said he sounded cute." Sabrina glanced over her shoulder and shrugged. "You weren't wrong."

"Suh-breen-nuh." Riley dragged out her name. "Hush."

"That's enough, girls. You're going to make our guest blush." Art chuckled. "This is Blake. He's returning Charlie's phone."

"And finishing the last brownie." Tori pointed to the crumbly evidence Blake had left behind on the island, the long sleeve of her hand-me-down robe dangling almost to her fingers.

"Oh, I'm sorry, did you want that?" Blake stepped forward, and for a second, Charlie wondered if he was going to offer the younger girl his used napkin full of crumbs.

He stopped midstride toward the island as Tori shook her head. "We're not allowed to have sugar after 8:00 p.m., anyway."

"*And* Mr. Blake is our guest." Gretchen's soothing voice eased the edge of Charlie's nerves. "Remember how we treat guests?"

The teens mumbled their acknowledgment, a varied chorus of *yes ma'am*s. One of the lessons Gretchen had taught Charlie in high school, which the older woman still preached today with the incoming and outgoing foster teens, was putting others' needs ahead of their own. Maybe that was why Blake's selfishness—then *and* now—rubbed so wrong. It'd been ingrained in Charlie to be considerate, to sacrifice, to love others more than herself...so to have someone dear to her not return the favor had been detrimental.

The Bible clearly said love wasn't arrogant, that it was patient and that it didn't insist on its own way—which led Charlie to one obvious conclusion.

Blake had never truly loved her.

Tori crept up beside Charlie and leaned against her arm. "We'll just say good-night again."

"Good night again." The wave of melancholy faded as Charlie wrapped her arm around Tori and her fluffy purple robe and squeezed. Being a CASA volunteer had been one of the best decisions she'd ever made. The teens at Tulip House always lifted her spirits—especially Tori with her kindness and innocence. Despite her hard knocks in life, the younger girl hadn't succumbed to bitterness.

Maybe Charlie still needed to learn from them as much as they needed to learn from her.

"We're going back to bed." Riley tugged Sabrina's arm. "Good night, everyone."

Sabrina wiggled her fingers at Blake, who had finally managed to scoot past the teens and was making a beeline toward the breakfast nook and Art. Riley pulled Sabrina back into the hallway to head to their shared room.

"Hey, tomorrow's Saturday!" Tori pushed her messy blond hair out of her face. "Are we making cinnamon rolls?"

"Of course." Art pulled out the chair next to him as Blake neared the table. "That is, if you girls still want to help." He nodded at her and Nadia.

"Of course," Tori repeated. She leaned back into Charlie's side. "Are you coming?"

"Of course," Charlie echoed back. "You know I never miss cinnamon rolls." She'd spent the later part of her teen years side by side with Art in the kitchen, learning baking techniques she'd later experimented with and perfected on her own. He was largely part of why she'd grown interested in her trade and started Flour Power.

Blake sat down, his shoulders stiff, and Gretchen smiled at him. "These ladies sure are learning their way around a kitchen. Art's been teaching them the ropes, just like he did with Charlie. We'll have to have you over for a homemade dinner before you leave town."

Charlie shook her head and widened her eyes at Gretchen.

"Of course." Using the same phrase they'd all just used, Blake nodded at Gretchen, who promptly lit up like a Christmas tree.

Nadia rolled her eyes. "This family needs a thesaurus."

And Gretchen, oblivious to—or perhaps just in denial of—Charlie's distress, beamed. "Great! In fact, why wait? There'll be plenty of cinnamon rolls in the morning. You can come then."

"No!"

Everyone turned to Charlie, and only then did she realize she'd said the word out loud. She cleared her throat. "I mean, I'm sure Blake has a ton of stuff to do for work tomorrow. We wouldn't want to put him on the spot."

He rubbed the back of his neck and shrugged, the motion making him look much more like the younger Blake she remembered from high school. Boyish, hesitant, kind Blake—before he'd run away. "Actually, I'm sort of at a standstill until Monday."

Because of the mix-up at the shelter regarding the owner, Charlie was sure. He'd have to dig into county records to find out the current landowner was Mark Raines. Of course, if she gave him the information he needed, he could move forward sooner…

Doing so would help her avoid seeing him this weekend, but it would only provide aid in the war she was ultimately trying to win. And there was still the lingering question as to why he'd even want to come for breakfast in the first place. What was his agenda?

She used to be able to read Blake, her former best

friend, at a glance, but now—it was as if a brick wall had replaced any previous transparency. She studied his thick dark hair, his mature jaw, the familiar dimple in his chin that he used to be so embarrassed about but that she always found incredibly endearing, and her heart threatened to tumble.

Very confusing, looking at someone you once knew better than you knew yourself, and only seeing a stranger.

"Then it's set." Art's voice was commanding in the cozy kitchen space. Charlie jumped. "Cinnamon rolls in the morning, nine o'clock. Come hungry, son—we don't skimp here at the Tulip House."

"No, but we sure coupon." Gretchen laughed.

"Do you have any food allergies?" Tori squinted at Blake.

He shook his head. "I don't think so." Then he attempted an awkward grin. "Guess we'll find out, huh?"

Tori crossed her arms, her expression serious. "Food allergies aren't a joke."

Blake's face paled beneath his thickening five o'clock shadow. "I'm so sorry. Is someone here allergic to something?"

"No." Nadia lightly thumped Tori's arm through her robe. "She's kidding."

"I was making a joke," Tori admitted. "Sorry."

"No, don't apologize. It was funny." Blake stood up quickly, knocking his chair over. "I do need to be going, though. Thanks for the coffee, Gretchen." He shook Art's hand, then practically bolted for the front door. "Good night, everyone. See you tomorrow."

The door shut behind him with a sturdy click.

Gretchen, Art, Nadia and Tori all turned and stared directly at Charlie.

"What?" She busied herself gathering their used mugs for the sink. Except she knew what. She knew *exactly* what.

Gretchen pointed toward the front yard. "Go talk to him. He clearly felt uncomfortable."

"He *should* feel uncomfortable. He's—" She glanced at Tori and Nadia, then stopped. She didn't want the teens to know about Paradise Paws yet. Not until the danger was behind them. "You know."

Nadia brought the remaining mugs to the sink. "But remember how we treat our guests?" Her voice singsonged with amusement.

Tori frowned. "I don't get it."

"You will." Nadia patted her head, laughing as Tori ducked out from beneath the condescending gesture. "Just wait."

"It's *not* what you're thinking." Charlie turned her back to the sink full of dirty dishes and discovered four sets of eyes still aimed directly at her. "Okay, fine, I'll go out there. But no promises as to what I'll say."

Gretchen handed Charlie her coat she'd left hanging by the front door. "Take your time."

"Look, if you're going to survive the Tulip House visit, you've got to stop freezing up every time the teens talk to you."

The slamming door punctuated the statement, and Blake turned from his car to face the female force striding toward him across the winter lawn. So close. He'd been a foot from his car—more specifically, from escape.

He let out a long breath into the chilly night air. "What do you mean?"

Not that he needed to ask. Charlie would make her opinion known regardless.

"The way you interact with the girls—both times today, especially Tori. You're so nervous with them." Charlie crossed her arms over her sweatshirt. "They don't bite, you know."

He wasn't entirely convinced Charlie wouldn't.

He eased back a step. "I never thought they did." He wasn't scared of the teenagers—slightly intimidated, yes. The pressure was high, and Charlie had no idea the panicked thoughts that raced through his mind every time Tori walked into the view. *That's your niece—your flesh and blood you never even knew about. She even looks like your family— what if someone notices? What if she doesn't like you?*

And the loudest one of all. *What if you're not fit to be a father figure?*

"You probably should get it together before breakfast tomorrow. Although I have no idea why you're coming back in the first place." Charlie shivered, despite the oversize jacket wrapped around her small frame. "You seemed really uncomfortable in there."

Why was he coming? Because his niece lived there. Because he needed to get know her before he sprang potentially life-changing news on her…because he really wanted it to be *good* news when she learned who he was.

And maybe mostly because he needed to prove to the Jolies—and to Charlie—that he wasn't the same man who left town years ago. And eating cinnamon rolls with his niece and trying to get his head wrapped around all this seemed an organic segue into showing all of them that he wasn't a monster trying to take away a dog shelter. He was a man on a mission.

But he couldn't tell Charlie any of that right now.

So he unwound his scarf and draped it around her neck.

Surprise lit her expression. She tugged the ends of the

scarf, straightening it and mashing her hair flat against her shoulders. "Thank you."

He fought the urge to reach out and free her hair from the fabric trap. This rogue part of him that wanted to be familiar with her again was going to get him in trouble. Those days were over.

"You're welcome." He flipped the collar of his jacket up against the sudden rush of wind that skittered the bare tree limbs overhead and enjoyed the moment of peace.

"So...why are you coming?"

Definitely part bulldog. She couldn't let anything go. "Because I was invited, and it's rude to disrespect the woman who invested in me years ago."

"Eight years ago." Charlie tucked her chin into the scarf, her big brown eyes holding his as she clarified.

"It's been a long time," Blake admitted. "Not much has changed, though."

"And a lot of other things have."

Blake shoved his hands into his coat pockets. "Look, I get that you're mad at me and you've declared me the bad guy. This isn't an ideal situation."

"I'll say."

Sudden motion at one of the house's windows caught his attention. Blake squinted toward the brick structure. Two pairs of eyes—at two different heights—peered through the blinds.

"Looks like we have an audience." Blake chuckled.

Charlie whipped her head toward the house and pointed at the window. The blinds snapped shut, and the light clicked off. She shook her head, a smile softening the tension in her expression. "They don't get a lot of visitors."

"How long have they all lived here?" He held his breath, wanting all the details about Tori he could possibly get without raising suspicion. Of course, her case-worker, Anita, had given him a myriad of facts when they talked earlier that afternoon, but he had a sense Charlie knew a lot more about Tori's day-to-day life.

"Tulip House opened roughly two years ago. Gretchen and Art had always fostered—as you know with me—but they felt led to start an official home for multiple kids at a time, specifically teens. They thought the group dynamic could open new ministry opportunities and give the girls more instant friendships and support."

Charlie hunched into her jacket as she looked back at the two-story house behind her. A light snow began to fall, dusting her shoulders and hair with flakes of white. "Nadia came a little over a year ago. Last Christmas was her first one here, and it was rough. She's come a long way."

She tilted her head and rolled in her lip, as if considering an invisible calendar. "Sabrina and Riley are fraternal twins—they've been in the system several years now and, so far, have managed to stay placed together. They came to Tulip House about nine months ago. And Tori is our new girl. She's only about four months in."

He already knew the answer, but he had to ask anyway—just to be sure. "Where did she come from?"

"A facility across state that was closing."

"Was she there most of her life?"

"No, she's hopped around a little. And it was a temporary placement, anyway." Charlie scuffed one boot against the concrete driveway, as if the conversation pained her. "She was in one family home for several years, but she's never been clear to adopt. The family had to move on and take another child who was."

How horrifically traumatic. Blake's stomach twisted. "Why wasn't she clear?"

Charlie lifted one shoulder. "Something about attempting to contact next of kin but never being able to find them."

That would be him—he was the next of kin. He pulled in a tight breath, pressure pounding behind his eyes. He'd changed his name to distance himself from his father, making the caseworker's attempts at contact nearly impossible. It'd been amazing that they ever did. If he'd not made such a drastic move for himself, he could have been notified years ago. Tori's life could have been so different—so much more secure.

Charlie side-eyed him, interrupting his runaway thoughts. Snow fluttered off her eyelashes. "I'm not declaring you the bad guy, by the way. The girls don't know anything about the animal shelter yet."

"Good." Relief thundered through his bones, and he stomped his feet for warmth. "Thank you for that." The last thing he needed was for Tori to think he was the enemy—and clearly, Charlie had influence over the younger girl. Anything she said would go a long way, for better or for worse.

And a tiny piece of his heart he thought long dormant really wanted this fiery redhead in front of him to not think he was so awful, either.

He drew a hopeful breath, careful to keep his tone level. Something about being back in Tulip Mound made him care much more than he should. He and Charlie were history. And yet…

"So, you don't think I'm a bad guy?"

Charlie lifted her chin. "I said I wasn't *declaring* it. You've announced it loud and clear for everyone all on your own." Then, with more sadness in her eyes than anger, she handed over his scarf and walked back to the house.

Chapter Six

Three cinnamon rolls, two cups of coffee and one allegedly pulled muscle later, Charlie found herself standing in Tulip Mound's favorite—and only—Christmas tree farm. The snow was nearly up to her ankles and her stress was up to *here*, but she pasted on a smile, determined not to ruin the festive event for Nadia and Tori.

Tori pulled her purple gloves out of her coat pocket and put them on. "Do you think Papa Art will be okay?"

"Oh, I'm *sure* he'll be fine." Considering how the pulled muscle in his shoulder had conveniently occurred after Gretchen had not-so-subtly hinted they should go get their Christmas tree for Tulip House today, she was more than certain he'd be fully recovered and chopping firewood by the time they got back.

Blake shot Charlie an amused glance, like the ones they used to share all the time in high school over homework notes and inside jokes. He'd apparently picked up on it, too. Charlie had no idea what Gretchen was up to—either matchmaking or forcing reconciliation—but either way, she needed to stop. It wasn't going to happen. Blake had seen to that years ago by abandoning her, and then by returning not to seek her out or apologize, but to dismantle the only animal rescue in town.

He was the enemy—even if he did look incredibly handsome in a green thermal that made his blue eyes that much richer.

Nadia sidestepped a family in matching buffalo-plaid jackets pulling their Christmas tree on a sled and cast a wary glance around the fenced-in "forest."

"Did anyone get measurements for this thing?"

"We need a six- or seven-foot tree," Blake answered. "Their ceilings aren't tall, and we need to save room for the topper."

Charlie raised her eyebrows at him. How did he know that?

He caught her stare and shrugged, as if reading her mind. "Common sense. Plus, I remember Gretchen's giant star topper years ago." He offered a grin, one that felt like a truce.

For a moment, temptation tugged. It would be nice to let her guard down, pick out a tree and have fun with her long-lost best friend. But there could be no truce where there was no compromise. And if Blake was still lingering in Tulip Mound for the sole purpose of buying Paradise Paws out from under them all, she couldn't afford to relax. Especially since she couldn't tell the girls what Blake was really in town to do without risk of ruining their Christmas.

She cleared her throat. "Gretchen got a new topper a few years ago, but yes, good idea. We'll still need to save room." An irrational part of her wanted to add, *If you'd been here past eight years, you'd know that.* She bit down on her lower lip to stop the flow of emotion. It was just a tree topper—it didn't matter.

So why did it suddenly feel like so much more than that?

They started searching the rows of snow-dusted trees, the frozen ground crunching under their boots as they walked. Nadia grudgingly lagged a few steps behind, while Tori strode eagerly ahead, leaving Blake and Charlie to awkwardly walk side by side. She kept her hands in her pockets, lest they accidentally graze Blake's. It was all she could do not to let her mind wander down memory lane as they strolled through the tree farm—whimsical, once-upon-a-time type thoughts of all the past Christmases spent with Blake.

Wrapping-paper wars to see who could decorate a gift the fastest. Taste testing her latest Christmas creations in the Jolies' kitchen. Helping Art hang lights on the outside of Tulip House—before it was even called that.

For years, Blake's presence had dominated every Christmas memory. Caroling the town with fellow church members. His elbow warm against her side as they all pressed into the pew on Christmas Eve night.

Her stomach twisted. At least this year, he'd be back in Colorado before the actual holiday arrived. Having him here—but not in the form of the Blake she used to love—could prove more painful than all the years he'd been absent.

"What about a little one?" Tori's voice broke through her thoughts. "Like in that holiday cartoon with Snoopy?"

Charlie blinked, then focused back on the teens as Tori pointed to a short, scraggly tree, its thin branches barely offering any green.

Nadia snorted. "That's literally the opposite of what we're looking for."

Tori reached out and gently touched the end of a bare limb. "I think it's cute."

"We'll take it," Blake declared.

"What?" Nadia gaped.

"Yeah, what?" Charlie echoed.

He checked the price-per-foot chart a staffer had handed them when they entered the farm a few minutes earlier. "Why not? It's cheap."

"There's no way Mama Gretchen is going to want that in her living room." Nadia crossed her arms over her red coat.

Tori frowned. "You're not the boss."

Charlie put her hand on each of their shoulders. "Come on. Let's go find one we *all* like that will get the job done."

Tori sighed but didn't protest as they continued down the rows toward the grander trees.

Blake kept side-eyeing Tori, as if hating to see her disappointed. Charlie held back, studying him as he studied the younger girl, and couldn't help but wonder if he'd ever wanted to be a dad. Was he seeing anyone in Colorado? She had no idea what his life—or his relationships—had been these past several years. And while they'd never been more than best friends, her heart had stowed away with him when he disappeared. It'd taken almost a decade, but she'd finally thought she'd gotten it all back.

But now, walking beside Blake through a winter wonderland of Christmas trees, she wondered if there was still a piece of it tucked away in his coat pocket.

"Want to race?" Tori asked Nadia hopefully as the crowd thinned and they continued down the trail of trees.

Nadia rolled her eyes, the patronizing look almost lost in her fake eyelashes. "I'm not wearing the right shoes." She gestured to her heavy snow boots.

"Good. Then I'll be more likely to win." Tori pointed.

"Up that hill to that really tall tree. Ready? Go!" She took off in a sprint, snow flying up behind her own tan boots as her feet sought traction on the powdery ground.

"Ugh, fine." Nadia sighed, but a grin lingered behind the faux frustration as she dug in and took off after the younger girl. Snow sprayed in her wake. Both girls shrieked and ran faster, laughing as they fought to be the first to the big spruce.

"They seem to get along pretty good," Blake commented as they trailed after them.

Charlie took off her hat to brush her hair back from her face. "It depends."

"On what?"

"Honestly? Nadia's mood. She's sixteen and has been through the wringer." Charlie shrugged as she pulled her hat back on. "But here lately, they seem to be bonding a little better. Acting more like true sisters—one minute pretty close, the next on each other's nerves."

Blake quieted. "That must be nice."

"How is your sister?" He'd rarely ever talked about her, always changing the subject when Charlie used to question. In fact, she just now realized she'd never even known her name. "What's her name?"

"Danielle." He nodded, the motion crisp and not inviting any further conversation.

Which wasn't surprising. Blake had never talked much about his late mom, his gruff father or his sister. He'd just jumped into the family formed for her—Art and Gretchen—and hung around like one of them.

Until he didn't.

Her back stiffened. She'd forgiven him, but the hurt flared fresh every time she dared to glance into his deep blue gaze. So many disappointments—too many to name.

But if she started with the biggest, it'd be the abandonment of all that could have been. And all because he'd been in a hurry to leave Tulip Mound? He hadn't given a single thought to her when he'd made his ludicrous suggestion and then bailed.

And now, he still wasn't giving her—or her dreams—any consideration. Charlie glanced at his profile, impossible to read, and not because of the permanent five o'clock shadow he wore. She'd made a local name for herself in Tulip Mound with Flour Power, which obviously included her love for dogs. When Blake hadn't been there, the rescue shelter had. Rachel, several years her senior, had let Charlie come volunteer when she needed to feel connected to something…to someone who got it.

And those abandoned animals understood—which was exactly why Paradise Paws drew Nadia, Tori and the rest of the teens that filtered through Tulip House. Charlie wasn't sure who needed whom more—the teens or the dogs.

And now it was all at risk.

"I better go check on the girls." Charlie gestured up the path as she increased her pace. Not that she was deliberately trying to get away from Blake. But with her thoughts—and emotions—askew, a little distance wouldn't hurt. The last thing she needed was for Blake to pick up on her musings and think she still had a thing for him.

That was also the *very* last thing she needed her heart to think.

He'd missed it here.

Blake had tried to deny that fact. After the stress of the airport and securing his rental car the other day, he hadn't felt much when he saw the kitschy Welcome to Tulip Mound sign on his way into town.

He'd also denied that truth while checking in to the Hummingbird Inn—the only B&B in Tulip Mound without driving thirty minutes farther into Kansas City—and making small talk with owner Noah Montgomery. Noah had inherited the inn from his parents and had never missed a Sunday in the choir at Grace First Church as far back as Blake could remember.

It'd been harder to deny it while munching homemade cinnamon rolls this morning in Gretchen's kitchen, shifting under the heavy weight of Art's steady watch and trying to catch all his crumbs before they hit the kitchen floor.

But slinging a snowball into Charlie's pale blue fleece–covered back…well, he couldn't deny it anymore. He'd missed a lot of things about home—but he never missed a well-aimed shot.

Charlie shrieked, her back arching as fragments of snow found their way down her jacket. She whirled around, hat askew, her eyes wide as she searched for her attacker. Her gaze landed on his, and a tiny part of him seized up with terror.

The other part of him bent down to scoop snow and reload.

"Don't you dare." She pointed with a gloved hand, and he grinned. Suddenly, he wasn't Blake Bryant, corporate liaison. He wasn't here to broker a deal or negotiate funds.

He was just a guy aiming a snowball at his best friend.

He held up his second shot. With surprising speed, she stooped down and packed her own snowball. He still could have taken her down, but he waited, eager to see how this would play out. She took aim, and he rushed toward a tree off the path.

"No fair hiding." She wielded her icy weapon. "I should get at least one shot at you."

The weight of the words clamored to land in his heart. She'd *had* a shot with him—the same night of his ultimate falling-out with his dad, when he'd asked her to come back to Kansas City with him.

She'd said no.

Charlie bringing up his sister a few minutes ago had reminded him of how much of his story Charlie still didn't know, despite their close relationship in the past. And he couldn't tell her any of it now without telling her the whole thing. In a nutshell? Danielle had lied about having a miscarriage. And, in doing so, had started a chain reaction of consequences that she continued to live out in jail.

His arm lowered slightly, and Charlie took her chance. The snowball hit the center of his chest. She'd always had a way of aiming straight at his heart. He hesitated, battling the temptation to let that arrow sink in and walk away wounded. But the clouds overhead parted, and the snow glistening in Charlie's red hair begged for more companions.

He gathered more powder and took aim. She squealed and ran for a tree. He took off after her, his brain begging him to have some dignity and not literally chase the woman who'd turned him down. But the desire to have fun, to forget about his family dysfunction and enjoy the moment took precedence, and he obeyed it as he slung around the trunk of a spruce.

Charlie held up one hand in surrender, and he lowered his snowball—unfortunately, before he could fully register the fact that her other hand had been hidden behind her back.

Cold, slushy ice slid down his throat and into the neck of his thermal shirt. He fought to save face and contain his reactionary gasp, at once amused and appreciative of the victory spark lighting Charlie's eyes as she backed away. She'd always been *so* competitive.

Which was the only reason why he did what he did next. He dropped the snowball he held straight on top of her head.

She shrieked as she turned to run—but her boot caught on a fallen branch, and she went down on both knees. Blake tripped over her sprawled legs, and he landed hard next to her, snow sinking into the tops of his shoes and soaking through the front of his shirt.

Laughing, he struggled to right himself. He rolled toward her to sit up, just as she propped up on one elbow next to him. His breath hitched at the sudden proximity, and a million memories of similar moments assaulted him so much harder than packed ice, one after the after.

Him and Charlie, heads ducked low together in Gretchen's kitchen as they shaped dough for Charlie's latest baking creation. Him and Charlie, sharing a bucket of popcorn at the movie theater and batting each other's hands away from the extra-buttery pieces. Him and Charlie, perched in Farmer Benton's field on a truck tailgate, identifying constellations for her sophomore-year project.

Blake swallowed, forcing himself to ease back a few inches instead of obeying the magnetic field tugging him toward her—his true north. "Are you okay?"

She brushed snow off her face, but the effort was wasted due to the amount of powder coating her gloves. "I think so." Her eyes looked a little dazed, and he didn't think it was from the sudden fall. Was she remembering, too?

He couldn't fight the attraction—or their past connection—any longer. They'd been voted "most likely to end up together" in their high school yearbook for a reason. If he had any regrets with Charlie, one of the top ones had to be that he'd never kissed her.

Could he leave Tulip Mound again carrying the same one?

He leaned in an inch, then two, his eyes seeking hers. She wasn't moving closer or away—rather, she seemed frozen, her gaze ping-ponging between his eyes and his lips.

He was the enemy. They both knew it. But there was something still tying them together despite their current obstacles—a bridge he knew they could somehow cross if they both just took a few steps. He closed the distance between them another inch, close enough to see the snowflakes competing with the freckles on her cheeks. He slowly reached up to brush them off.

"I won!"

Blake jerked back, lowering his hand just as Nadia and Tori appeared at the top of the trail, out of breath.

"I won," Tori announced again. Then her eyes narrowed in suspicion as she took in the two of them sitting on the ground covered in snow.

Nadia squinted at them, too, a knowing smirk on her lips. "So, who won *this* battle?"

"Actually, it's not over yet." Still sitting, Blake scooped more powder and lobbed it at Nadia, who neatly sidestepped the attempt.

"Amateurs." She tugged off her gloves, shoved them in her coat pocket and then began to pack a perfectly round snowball.

Uh-oh. Blake scrambled to his feet, grabbing Charlie's arm and hauling her upright. That'd been close. Too close. He bit back a groan. Had he really almost kissed her? Charlie would have probably smacked him—and not with snow.

Despite the disappointment looming over him, he had to admit it was for the best they'd been interrupted. He didn't need any more complications when he left Tulip Mound. He wasn't here for Charlie, as much as memory lane beckoned. He was here for his niece.

Not wanting Tori to be left out of the fight, he ducked down to make another snowball just as Nadia released hers. It sailed over his head and smacked the tree. Snow scattered in all directions.

Tori tossed one at Charlie and missed. "Can't get me!"

"Just wait." Charlie began to make a snowball. Was she avoiding Blake's eyes? What was she thinking?

Too much to figure out now. Besides, Tori waited.

"She might not be able to, but I can!" Blake quickly formed a ball as Tori began to run toward the trees, giggling. He took aim at her retreating, jacket-clad back.

Tori spun around at the last second, her mouth open as she laughed. Then her eyes widened as the snowball slammed straight into her face.

So much for bonding.

Chapter Seven

Charlie handed Sabrina the next ornament in line for positioning on the tree in Gretchen's living room. "Looks like there's an open spot next to the big Mickey Mouse, there."

Sabrina passed the dangling snowflake ornament over to Riley, who carefully tucked the decoration into the branches.

"You never could stand for there to be a hole." Gretchen smiled at Charlie as she lifted the lid from the next box of ornaments. They'd rarely created themed trees over the holidays at Tulip House, preferring instead to decorate with an eclectic, nostalgic arrangement of ornaments collected over the years. Each Thanksgiving, whoever was staying at Tulip House carried on the tradition Art and Gretchen had started when Charlie first came into their home at the age of fourteen—picking out a new ornament for the tree and writing their name on the bottom.

"There's something so magical when the tree is completely full to bursting." Charlie's return grin fell as a new memory rose to the surface. That last Thanksgiving before Blake left town, he'd picked an ornament to contribute to Art and Gretchen's tree.

And never got to hang it.

"Hey, Charlie, this one is yours from last year." Tori, her nose still swollen, and her eye tinged with light purple from the snowball fight, handed Charlie a miniature baking sheet full of cookies hanging from a small hook.

"Thanks, Tori." She took the ornament, then brushed the girl's hair gently back from her face. She winced at the bruise. "Do you need more ice?"

"I think she got plenty of that at the tree farm." Nadia snorted as she adjusted a string of garland draped among the branches.

"Nadia." Gretchen's gentle reprimand held as much humor as correction.

"I'm just saying." She spread her hands wide in alleged innocence before dipping back into the box.

"It doesn't hurt that bad anymore." Tori rummaged through the tin, her hair falling back against her face and effectively hiding her from further comment.

"It was an accident," Gretchen reminded Nadia.

"You weren't there." Sabrina raised her eyebrows at the house mother. "Can you say for sure?"

"Sabrina!" Riley elbowed her sister in the ribs. "I really don't think Blake would have hurt Tori on purpose."

"But you don't know him. None of us do." She gestured around the room with the candy cane ornament in her hand before her gaze landed on Charlie. "Except her, apparently."

"They used to date," Nadia eagerly supplied.

That hit like a sucker punch. Charlie hauled in her breath. "Girls, we—"

"Blake and Charlie are just good friends from way back." Gretchen's tone left no room for argument. "That's all there is to that story."

That was all to the end of it, anyway. Were the details

along the way even worth remembering at this point? But Gretchen's abrupt summation of one of the most important relationships in Charlie's life left her feeling slightly off-kilter. Gretchen was right. Good friends.

So why did that truth sting fresh?

And where *was* Blake, anyway? He'd dropped them at Tulip House with the tree they'd picked out, made sure Art didn't need any help and that Tori had an ice pack, then vanished.

Maybe the better question to ask was—why did she notice or care? Charlie tried to put aside her anger. It was Christmastime. The teens were none the wiser to his involvement with the shelter. Right now, they didn't even know Paradise Paws was in danger of shutting down— and she'd like to keep it that way for as long as possible.

"Girls, let me get a quick picture of all of you with your new ornaments." Gretchen waved the four teens together, despite their mostly unanimous moans of protest. Only Tori seemed interested, shuffling toward the center of the tree in her house shoes, new ornament in hand.

"Now hold them up and say, 'snow globe'!" Gretchen instructed. Then she lowered her phone and pursed her lips in mild frustration. "Nadia, I said, 'say, "snow globe."' Not 'ear lobe.'"

Sudden knocking sounded on the front door. Art, who'd escaped to the kitchen to avoid the decorating chaos, hollered, "I'll get it!"

Gretchen coaxed another picture out of the girls, then urged Charlie into the shot. She leaned in with the teens, holding up her baking sheet ornament, briefly wondering where the one Blake had purchased years ago had gone. Had he taken it with him? Maybe it'd gotten thrown away.

Or maybe Gretchen had hidden it, knowing how badly

it'd hurt to see it that first year in his absence. She'd never even known what it was.

"What's this?" Art's voice boomed from the foyer. Low voices and then the slight rustling of branches followed.

Blake appeared in the living room, Tori's scraggly Charlie Brown tree in hand. His hair, dark and still damp from the snow, was tousled, as if he'd tried to fix it before he'd walked in. He offered a tentative smile, his gaze lingering on Charlie before landing on Tori. "Surprise."

Charlie's heart dipped as Tori lit up like—well, like a Christmas tree—and rushed toward Blake. "Is this for me?"

"It sure is. I figure it's the least I can do after the snowball accident." He set the tree on the ground and straightened, the top of the tree barely coming to his hip. It'd be the perfect size for Tori's room.

"I've never had my own tree before." She stared at it like it was made of gold and not barely holding itself together on Gretchen's worn carpet.

"That's really nice, Blake." Gretchen joined them, touching the nearly bare limbs. "You didn't have to, you know. Tori understands this was an accident."

"It's not a problem," Blake assured them. "If you point me in the right direction, I'll get this set up."

"This way!" Tori paraded down the hall, leading the way to her room. Sabrina and Riley shared, but Gretchen had always tried to keep a single room for the oldest girl in Tulip House. Right now, that was Nadia, which meant Tori had her own room by default. The next girl who came into the house would end up bunking with Tori, unless Nadia aged out first.

Charlie began to put the lid on the ornament tub as Gretchen and the other girls filed down the hall, whispering as they followed Tori and Blake. She didn't want to join them. Seeing Blake up close, the contented look on his face as he took in Tori's joy…it was beyond confusing. Why would he do such a nice thing when he was in the process of doing such a horrible one behind the scenes? Did he not realize how the teens would be affected if the shelter closed?

"It's a nice gesture." Art leaned against the door frame separating the hallway from the living room and crossed his arms over his faded college football sweatshirt. "You've got to admit."

"It is." The admission could have been pried more easily from her mouth with pliers. Charlie took a deep breath and picked up her baking sheet ornament again. "It's just…"

"Complicated?" Art asked.

She traced the outline of the miniature cookie tray. "That's one word for it."

Art brushed his hand through his salt-and-pepper hair and gave her the fatherly smile that came so naturally for him. "It's like a recipe." He pointed to the ornament in her hand. "Lots of ingredients, and it takes time to rise."

Charlie made her way to the Christmas tree and searched for the right branch to hang the little tray on. "What's like a recipe?"

"Love, of course."

She nearly dropped the ornament. She hooked it on the branch, her fingers trembling. "Who said anything about love?" Charlie balked. "He's just a guy…with a tree."

But minimizing the truth didn't make it go away. He wasn't just a guy. Blake was a *man*—her former best friend—who'd been the only one she'd allowed full access to her heart. The handful of dates she'd been on in the last several years had been one and done. None of them made her feel the way he had.

And, honestly, there wasn't room in her heart yet for someone else.

She paused, standing back to admire the tree and give herself time to process. "It's weird meshing the Blake I knew—"

"And loved," Art pointed out.

She shot him a look but didn't confirm. "—with the Blake that's here today. There's this odd disconnect. Like I'm remembering someone totally different."

"He grew up." Art pushed off from the door frame and walked closer to the tree. "You're probably different in a lot of ways to him, too. That's how it goes. Doesn't mean you two can't find your way to a friendship again."

Or to more. The unspoken hint floated between them in the living room like glitter in a snow globe. She *knew* he and Gretchen had been matchmaking earlier and not simply pushing for reconciliation.

"Well, I hate to disappoint you." Charlie brushed loose pine needles off her hands and her jeans. "But Blake and I making amends would take a Christmas miracle."

Art winked. "Good thing I know Who to go to for one of those."

Blake might have grown up with an older sister, but he was far from prepared for the drama that awaited him in the pink-ruffled bedroom in Tulip House.

It'd all begun smoothly enough. He'd toted the tree to Tori's room, where she proceeded to pick various spots for him to set it and then change her mind, over and over, until her entire room was rearranged and eventually put back the way it'd been. He'd finally set the tree in the corner, near the window, as Tori gleefully announced it was perfect.

Gretchen had gone for a tree stand and some twinkle

lights to string on the skinny, bare branches, and that was when trouble began.

"Would I get a tree, too, if you hit me in the face?" One of the twins—maybe Sabrina?—fake pouted, twirling one finger through her thick hair. Then again, he thought she was faking. It was hard to tell.

"Hush, Sabrina." The other twin reprimanded her. "You're just trying to cause trouble."

"She needs to stop." Nadia stepped closer to Sabrina, her tone mildly threatening.

Blake held up both hands. "You guys, Tori saw this tree earlier today and wanted it for Tulip House. That's all."

He hadn't meant to play favorites. At first, the idea to go back and get it for her had started with a measure of guilt that he'd tried to shake off, knowing accidents happened and they'd all just been having fun together.

But then the urge meshed into something deeper. When he thought about Tori's face as she'd fought for the tree to come to Tulip House, he recognized something in her expression. She wasn't just a kid asking for a new toy or something she liked. She *related* to the tree. It was smaller, like her. And unwanted, like she had to believe herself to be in her situation. That tree represented something much more important to her. It wasn't about Blake making up for a poorly aimed snowball.

It was about Blake making up for the past thirteen years of her life.

Unfortunately, no one else in the room saw it that way.

"And what if I don't stop?" Sabrina met Nadia toe-to-toe, her chin lifted despite her shorter stature. "What are you going to do?"

"Sabrina!" Riley chastised, tugging at her sister's arm. "Quit it. We're going to get kicked out if you fight again."

"We can get kicked out of Tulip House?" Tori's eyes widened, and she sank down on the edge of the twin-size bed.

"Of course." Sabrina snorted, crossing her arms over her chest. "Nothing in our life is permanent. You haven't figured that out yet?"

Tori's cheeks flushed red, and she gripped a pillow in her lap. "Then stop it! Both of you."

"Don't tell me what to do, teacher's pet." Sabrina reached over and jabbed Tori in the arm.

"Hey! That's enough." Blake's pulse roared in his ears. He hadn't meant to create trouble, and now Tori was taking the brunt of it.

"Back off. She's new." Nadia swatted at Sabrina, hard enough to mean business but not hard enough to hurt.

Sabrina didn't respond in kind. "Don't touch me." She shoved Nadia, both hands on the older girl's shoulders. Nadia stumbled backward, nearly tripping over a beanbag chair on the floor, then quickly regained her footing.

"Okay, that's it." Nadia cracked her knuckles, then dived onto Sabrina. The two girls fell to the carpet in a heap. Riley gasped and scrambled away. Tori pressed the pillow over her mouth and screamed.

Blake couldn't let them hurt each other. He reached for Nadia and tried to haul her off Sabrina, who'd lifted her arm in a threat. Nadia rolled to the left at the last minute, and Sabrina's hand slapped Blake square across the cheek instead.

He recoiled backward, shaking off the sting as he quickly rocked back on his heels out of the way. Nadia stood abruptly, and Sabrina's eyes widened as she scrambled upright, as if recognizing she'd gone too far. "Don't tell." Her panicked whisper filled the room. "Please."

Riley grabbed Blake's arm, her tone pleading. "Please, please, don't. I don't want to move again."

He looked at Nadia, who simply brushed back her braid and shrugged, looking away as if she'd had no part in this. Then he looked at Tori, who had moved to stand by the door, her hands covering most of her face.

He was in *way* over his head.

Blake took a deep breath and stood. "Okay, listen, all of you. No more picking on Tori. And no more fighting. Understand?" He tried to find his most intimidating, professional business voice, but he had a feeling he sounded more like a substitute teacher trying to call a class to order. At least Tori would be grateful he'd stood up for her— that'd be one good thing to come from this chaotic night.

He turned to face her, but her teary expression wasn't gratitude. In fact, her eyes filled with what could only be described as accusation. "Look what you did." She turned to run from the room but bumped squarely into Charlie and Art coming in.

"What's going on?" Art's tall frame filled the tiny bedroom. "We heard yelling."

Gretchen piled in right behind them. "What happened?" Her motherly concern stirred an ache Blake hadn't felt in over a decade. He pressed his fingers to his temple as his head began to pound. What was he doing here?

"Ask Tori." Nadia pointed, but the younger girl was already squeezing past Charlie and heading down the hall.

Blake held out one hand toward her, but she was gone. He slowly let his arm fall to his side, glancing over just in time to see disappointment welling in Charlie's gaze. She shook her head at him, then took off after Tori.

Zero for two.

Chapter Eight

❧

"Now they all have trees." Charlie sat on the back step of Paradise Paws, holding Cooper in her lap, and exhaled through her nose. "All four of them!"

Rachel pressed her lips together, but it didn't stop the smile sweeping across her face as she poured a bag of kibble into the outdoor food bucket. "You've got to admit, that's pretty cute. Mr. CEO from the big city buying all these foster teens their own Charlie Brown trees?"

"Don't even go there," Charlie warned. She stroked Cooper's fur. She'd brought him with her to visit Rachel at Paradise Paws Sunday afternoon for two reasons. One, he loved visiting the shelter where he'd spent several months of his life and playing with the other dogs awaiting adoption, and two, she knew she'd need his comfort while she hashed out yesterday's events.

She continued, "Blake is up to something. You don't swoop back into town and try to negotiate the closing of the only no-kill animal shelter around and then do something like that for no reason."

"Maybe he's trying to make up for it." Rachel shrugged,

pausing to brush her dark hair out of her face. "Maybe he feels bad about this potential deal."

"If he feels bad, then why pursue it?" Charlie asked. She shifted as the cold from the concrete stair began to seep through her jeans.

"Why does anyone do anything?" Rachel straightened from the bin of dog chow as she pointed at Charlie. "Actually, I'll tell you why people do things—for love, money or faith." She squinted. "Is he a believer?"

"He used to be." Charlie released Cooper as he squirmed to get down. "I don't know anything about him now." Except that he was really trying to bond with the kids at Tulip House. And that his interest in Gretchen and Art seemed genuine. And that he looked really good in dark green and hadn't struggled at all carrying their tree for them the other day and still had the ability to make her stomach dip when she let her guard down.

Okay, so she knew a few things.

"Is he a good kisser?" Rachel winked as she poured the last bowl.

Charlie narrowed her eyes. "I wouldn't know *that*, either."

"Not yet, anyway." Her friend smirked.

"Rachel! He's the enemy." Charlie's heart pounded just thinking about it. She'd almost told Rachel about that near kiss they'd shared at the tree farm but was glad now she hadn't. Especially not after last night's events. Clearly that near kiss had been a temporary lapse of judgment she'd narrowly escaped. "That's the last thing I'm wondering about."

Well, maybe second to last, if she were brutally honest. But it was far down on the list. The top item being, what was Blake *really* up to? A man didn't just suddenly move away and change his name without having a big reason to do so.

"I'm just saying, you've got a twinkle in your eye, and it's much too early in December for that to be Santa-related." Rachel pushed up her sweater sleeves and then joined Charlie on the top step.

Charlie scooted over to make room. "I think Gretchen is playing matchmaker, too, sending us for trees in the first place and then talking him up in front of me." After her conversation with Art last night and his suggestion of the *L* word, it seemed clear that Gretchen was pushing them together.

Rachel tilted her head. "I'm not going that far—I mean, the man is clearly an obstacle right now. But wasn't he really important to you once?"

"Once, yes. But people change." Blake sure had. But like Art said...so had she. Did Blake think some of the same negative things about her that she thought about him?

For some reason, that bothered her more than she wanted to admit.

She squirmed on the stair. She'd have to deal with that fact eventually, but for now...changing the subject was much easier. "Why are you not more worried about all of this?" Charlie gestured toward the open acreage behind the shelter, where at least ten dogs ran and play-fought or basked in the sunshine. Waffles, his long ears hanging practically to his knees, waddled after a ball another dog had abandoned, then plopped down beside it as if playing alone was too much effort. He was probably bored without Tori to play hide-and-seek with.

"I was. But this morning's sermon hit the spot." Rachel let out a slow sigh as she surveyed the property—the gentle slope of hills leading down to the pond, where a thin top layer of ice sparkled under the sun, the spattering of oak trees with limbs reaching to the heavens, the old storage shed where they kept yard supplies and donations of dog food. "At some point, I have to do my part and then just trust God."

"Trust God," Charlie repeated. The words were true. She *should* trust Him—and usually did. But with something this important, it was extra hard to relinquish the reins. Though, on second thought, did she even have them in the first place? "Why is that so much easier said than done?"

"It always is." Rachel whistled, and Waffles trotted over to her for a belly rub. "I also had an idea last night of how to do the said part."

"Oh?" Charlie watched as Cooper gnawed on a stick a few yards away. Usually being around the dogs released her tension, but right now, it seemed to all be collecting on her shoulders.

"We can't control whether or not Mr. Raines sells to Blake's company, right?" Rachel shot her a sideways glance as she scratched the dog under the chin. "But we *can* raise money to try to move elsewhere if the worst happens."

Charlie nodded slowly, reaching over to scratch the hound's ears. "Fund-raising." Her inner wheels began to turn. She and the teens at Tulip House could easily help run a few events to earn funds for Paradise Paws. It was Christmas—people were generally in a spirit of giving, especially to good causes.

Her hopes began to soar. "You know, that might actually work. What about a hot chocolate stand? We could put it outside the shelter in the front yard, have people come by and donate while seeing the property and the animals up close."

"That's a good idea." Rachel sat back, and Waffles ambled over to the food bowl. Cooper joined him, sniffing the kibble before stealing a bite. "There are a lot of dogs here needing homes, and people will respond better if they're seeing the need for themselves."

"Of course, one fund-raiser won't be enough on its own, but if we can start some momentum, maybe plan a few more over the holidays…" Charlie's voice trailed off as she imagined the possibilities. They would need serious cash to help the shelter relocate, but it went back to that trust thing again, didn't it? All they could do was their part.

Cooper came over and pressed against Rachel's leg, panting, his thick gray eyebrows lifting as if asking if she was going to pet him. She obliged, and when she stopped, he leaned on Charlie next.

"Spoiled," Rachel laughed. "I knew you two would make a good pair."

"I honestly can't remember not having him, and it's only been a few years." Charlie rubbed his fluffy gray back. "He's so sweet and personable, sometimes I wonder if he's truly a dog."

"That's some good marketing copy right there." Rachel raised her brow knowingly. "Testimonials from past adoptions. We could print flyers with quotes to hand out with the hot chocolate."

Excitement bubbled. "That's a great idea! And Christmas is the perfect time of year to surprise a kid with a pet. I'll work that in, too." That'd be great if they were able to take care of two proverbial birds with one stone—more adoptions, *and* funding for future rescues.

"Marketing is the best when you really believe in what you're selling." Rachel elbowed Charlie before she pulled herself to her feet. "I wonder if your big-city friend will be able to understand that."

Charlie stood as well, brushing at the damp back of her jeans. "If this fund-raiser goes well, then it won't matter what he thinks."

"Won't matter what who thinks?" The deep male voice was followed by a sneeze.

Charlie's heart simultaneously leaped and fell as she turned to face the open screen door.

Blake.

A dozen emotions flickered across Charlie's expression as she took in the sight of him. One or two he thought he might like—ones that reminded him of how she'd looked at him when he came back from college to take her to her senior prom. And how she'd looked at him right before he dunked her in the community pool every summer…and more recently, how she'd looked at him while reclined back in the snow, flakes dusting her eyelashes as he leaned in for what surely would have been his favorite regret to date.

But the rest of those flickers in her expression made him want to head right back to his car—and watch his back along the way.

"We have a doorbell at the front that rings back here," Rachel reminded him. He couldn't tell if that was just handy information for next time or the nice woman's attempt at being not so nice.

"I didn't catch that." He'd started sneezing immediately upon climbing the front stairs, so he'd probably missed it with his watery eyes. He decided not to respond with the obvious fact that they also had a dead bolt, if they didn't want people walking inside. "I heard voices out here, so I came to find you."

His gaze landed back on Charlie, but not so fast that he didn't catch the way Rachel's dark eyebrows shot up— and the corners of her lips with them.

She tugged her sweater over her jeans and eased past Blake to the screen door he'd just vacated. "I'll just leave you two to chat." She disappeared inside before Charlie's half-formed protest could fully escape her mouth.

She turned to face him, scooping up a dark gray dog and holding him tight against her chest. A barrier, to be sure. She buried her face in the dog's furry neck. "How'd you know I'd be here?"

"I went to Tulip House first. Gretchen told me." Plus, Charlie was dedicated. With her current obvious passions, she could only be a handful of places. And after sitting in the back row of the church service that morning, conviction had gnawed until he decided he had to make it right. He had to find her.

He took a deep breath. "We need to talk."

Wariness furrowed her brow, and she reluctantly set the dog on the ground. "I don't have long. I've got work to do."

So did he, but best not to remind her of that part. Despite a slight delay in having to contact his assistant back in Colorado for the right log-ins, he'd discovered relatively quickly via online records that the current landowner was Mark Raines. He'd debated waiting until Monday to call, but the greater risk was having his own boss call *him* first, and Blake wouldn't be able to provide a positive update. He'd taken the risk.

And failed. Apparently, Mr. Raines was tired of so-

licitors and had hired an impressively intimidating sec-
retary to screen his calls. Blake had barely been able to
get a word in edgewise.

He'd have to try again tomorrow. Hopefully the older
woman liked Mondays more than he did and would be
in a better place for him to convince her he was legit.

But first...

"It won't take long. There's just something you need
to know." He grasped her arm and led her farther away
from the rescue building, into the dry winter grass. Another dog with incredibly droopy ears bounded up to
him, and he sneezed three times in succession. "A little
help?" He pulled a tissue from the pocket of his slacks.

Charlie rolled her eyes, then pointed to a large bucket
of dog food closer to the porch stairs. "Waffles! Chow
time."

"Waffles?" That was unexpected.

She nodded. "Tori's favorite. She comes over here and
plays hide-and-seek with him—he can find her no matter where she hides. She never wins."

"That's...cute." And foreign to him, having a dog as
a friend. He'd always been allergic and never able to
get close enough to make a bond. He watched as Waffles changed direction, heading for the food, and Blake
winced. He must look like such a jerk—the man who
was allergic to dogs attempting to close down the shelter where they lived. But there was so much more to the
story if Charlie could just understand. The problem was,
she couldn't.

Because he couldn't tell it.

But this next part, he had to tell.

"Listen, about last night..." He crossed his arms over
his chest, then sniffed, stepping a few feet farther away

from the nearby canines. "What exactly did Tori tell you happened with the tree?"

"That Nadia got jealous, and it made her feel bad." Charlie frowned, following him as he backstepped a few more paces. "You didn't have to get them all trees, you know."

He finally stood still and shoved his hands in his pockets. "I know. But I wanted to. I created a problem and didn't want Tori taking the brunt of it."

"I understand, but those girls also need to know how to work out things like jealousy and envy in a healthy way. It's a lesson they'll need for their adult lives."

"Agreed." Blake let out a long sigh. "But don't they also need to know they're cared about and that sometimes people give gifts because they want to?"

"Was it?" Charlie challenged. "Just because you wanted to?"

"It was all for Tori." The admission slipped off his lips before he could censor. Confusion clouded Charlie's face, and he rushed to cover his tracks. "I mean, she's so much younger than the others, and she's the new girl. It just made sense to me to get her something she really wanted."

Charlie seemed to accept that answer with her brisk nod. "Look, I know it's hard. I wanted to buy them all gifts the first few months I volunteered, too. But they need consistency and discipline and life lessons more than they need material objects. For some of these teenagers, it's the first time they've had any of it."

"So, ideally—both," Blake countered. "Lessons and gifts."

"Ideally, yes."

"Well, that's not actually the whole story."

She hiked an eyebrow, silently coaxing him to continue.

He drew a deep breath, hoping he was making the right decision. If it was the wrong one, it could drive a wedge even further between him and Tori. "Sitting in church this morning, I realized I wasn't doing anyone any favors by not telling you or Gretchen what happened." And of the two, it seemed easier to tattle to Charlie.

"Wait a second. You were at church?" Surprise flashed across her face.

He hadn't been to church in Colorado in a while, but Charlie couldn't have known that. "Is it that shocking?"

"Yes. I mean, no. I didn't see you." She waved her hand, flustered, before crossing her arms over her stomach. "I just didn't expect that."

Well, he hadn't expected a lot of things—like nearly kissing her in a snowball fight and realizing that after only forty-eight hours back at home, it felt a lot like he'd never left.

In fact, being in Tulip Mound was what had fed his desire to go back to services. He realized he'd missed it. He'd kept up his prayer life on his own but hadn't invested in a church community back in Denver. He'd always blamed it on work and said he'd go "next week" until the months blurred into years.

It'd been…nice. Refreshing, even. And effective. The sermon had certainly hit home. But now that meant he had to take action. "During the sermon, I felt convicted." Blake hesitated a beat. "I thought I was doing the girls a favor by covering this news up, but they got into a fight."

Charlie closed her eyes, disappointment creasing her forehead. She opened her eyes, her tone flat. "Nadia?"

"And Sabrina."

"Who started it?"

"Nadia, technically." He rushed ahead. "I can't say Sabrina didn't have it coming, though. She really goaded her."

"And the other two?" Charlie's chin lifted and her eyes glazed, transforming her from the role of caring volunteer to probation officer.

"Riley and Tori just watched." And squealed—loudly. "I broke it off as fast as I could. They begged me not to tell. Something about not wanting to get separated at Christmas."

The hard look in Charlie's eyes softened, and he felt himself melting again just remembering the desperation in their voices. No kid should ever have to feel that way in their home. "That's not going to happen, is it?"

Charlie shook her head. "Not for something that brief, but I'm glad you told me. We've got to address it. If Nadia keeps this up—or Sabrina, for that matter—and the caseworkers get wind of it, there's a chance they could be moved. Gretchen wouldn't request it for something this minor, but if it turns into a habit…" She shrugged. "Her hands might be tied. Especially if it spills back over into school."

"So, is it? A habit?"

"Nadia hasn't reacted that way in a long while. The last time was at the high school—a girl teased her so relentlessly about living at Tulip House. Nadia had enough and finally swung at her. She missed, but the girl landed the first punch in return, so the teachers determined the other girl was the perpetrator and suspended her for two days. Nadia got a day of detention, was all. But it's in her file."

"She was standing up for Tori." Blake ran his hand

over his hair. "Sabrina was teasing her pretty hard, then challenged Nadia when she tried to put a stop to it. I don't blame Nadia for reacting."

"They have to learn there's a better way." Charlie pressed her fingers against the bridge of her nose. "I keep trying to tell her—use words, not fists. Defuse, not ignite. Find an adult."

"I imagine where they're from, adults can't always be trusted." Or, in his case, *found*. His stomach knotted again with guilt.

Charlie lowered her hand from her face, her gaze catching his with surprise. "You're right. That's a great point, and sometimes I forget it." She snorted. "Ironically."

Sometimes he did, too. Charlie fit so well with Gretchen and Art, he forgot they weren't her real family. That she'd grown up in the system before landing with them. No wonder the teens were so important to her—she was like them, once upon a time.

No wonder Tori clung so close.

And the way they were talking now, discussing the teens and potential discipline and what they needed on a heart level, well—it felt a lot like coparenting. Which was both very appealing and very confusing.

Blake stepped back another foot, even though his nose didn't itch anymore. "What are you going to do?"

"Tell Gretchen. I'm sure the two girls will get a warning, maybe extra chores. She won't go too hard on them, but there has to be a consequence." She squinted at him. "And they're going to know you told."

He nodded slowly. "I understand. It's unavoidable."

He'd been afraid of that. Hopefully it wouldn't cause any more distrust between him and Tori—or Nadia. Anyone who stood up for Tori like that was a champion in his book, and he hated the thought of the older teen being upset with him, too. But even if they were, he was doing the right thing.

After all, if he was hoping to officially parent Tori one day, wasn't this part of it—making hard decisions in the present for future reward?

He must have looked more down than he realized, because Charlie gently placed her hand on his arm. "Thank you for telling me."

"You're welcome." He opened his mouth to say more, then stopped. There was no point in pressing further— or pulling her into the hug he desperately wanted. So he just stood still, enjoying the warmth of her hand radiating through his thin button-down shirt.

"I can't believe I'm doing this, but I'll tell you something in return. Because it, too, is clearly inevitable." Charlie bit down on her lower lip, then exhaled sharply as she pulled her hand away. "The man you're looking to contact is Mark Raines."

Surprise started a slow burn in his stomach. She was helping him? Of course, the fact remained… "I actually already realized that, but thank you for the heads-up."

"You found him?"

Blake shrugged. "It's sort of what I do. It's not hard to research once you can access public records online."

She narrowed her eyes, a small smile hinting at the corner of her glossy lips. "Well, do those public records tell you how to get past Mrs. Hoffman?"

Blake ran his hand over his hair, wishing the brief sensation of Charlie's hand on his arm didn't linger so vividly. "She's quite the gatekeeper, isn't she? She sort of made me feel like I needed to head back to church immediately." He laughed.

"She's retired from the army and takes her part-time job for Mr. Raines very seriously." Charlie hesitated, then peered up at him with a pointed gaze. "She also takes her grandkids very, *very* seriously. She loves to chat about them if given the chance."

He started to respond, then realized Charlie was helping him—handing over the key to the gate keeping him from Mark Raines. Which brought up a new question. "But why would you—"

She reached up, effectively cutting him off as she pressed her hand against his chest. The touch burned like a brand—but then again, hadn't he always been hers?

"Just say thank you."

Chapter Nine

"You told him?" Gretchen's voice contained equal measures of surprise and admiration. She crossed her arms over the red-and-green apron she'd thrown on when she'd joined Charlie in the community kitchen a half hour ago.

Charlie stirred the cookie batter in her mixing bowl a little more aggressively than it required. "I did." She blew a tuft of hair out of her face that had slipped loose from her ponytail. She didn't regret her decision to give Blake the head start yesterday afternoon. She'd wanted to return the favor from him sharing that hard story about the girls. And besides, giving Blake what he needed would hopefully just make him go away faster.

Funny that a few days ago that thought brought more relief than it did today.

She stirred harder, continuing to rationalize her decision. "The faster he can get to Mr. Raines, the faster Mr. Raines can deny his offer and we can stop worrying about all this."

Gretchen nodded. "Or the faster Mr. Raines will agree to sell and you guys can figure out an alternative plan for the shelter."

"Or that." Charlie continued her frantic churning.

"You're going to get a cramp." Gretchen nudged her out of the way. "Give me that." She expertly began to turn the batter, years of training under Art's careful instruction coming into play.

Charlie stepped back, massaging her hand before donning an oven mitt. "Do you really think he'll sell?"

Gretchen began to pour the batter into the cookie molds Charlie had sanitized and laid on the counter. "I think anything can happen, and we should prepare for the worst while hoping for the best."

"How are you always so wise?" Charlie bent to check on the cookies in the industrial-size oven, the heat sending a rush of warmth over her already-flushed cheeks. "Yet, that piece of good advice doesn't exactly lower my anxiety level."

"Trust." Gretchen scooped some clinging batter from the bowl into the last Christmas tree–shaped mold. "Remember? You can't control it. So, trust the One who can."

"But how do I know that God will—" Charlie stopped the much-too-honest words before they could completely spill from her mouth. She pressed her lips together.

"How do you know God will do what you want?" A patient grin stretched across Gretchen's face. She rested one hip against the counter and pointed the dripping wooden spoon at Charlie. "That's easy. You don't."

She let out a long sigh. "You make it *sound* easy. It's not."

"God has a plan."

But what if it wasn't hers? Charlie closed her eyes briefly before transferring the cookie sheet of baked trees to a cooling rack. Surely God agreed that these dogs didn't need to be homeless—and that the bond the teens had with the sweet animals didn't need to be dismissed. It'd be hard enough on Tori if Waffles ever got adopted—it'd be unbearable to know he didn't have a safe home at all anymore.

But what if God didn't agree? What if His plan hurt?

It had before. It hurt growing up in the foster system, moving from place to place and having no security for most of her childhood. It hurt watching the girls at Tulip House living in the same situation and coming off the same path. And it hurt that Blake had walked out on her years ago—like almost everyone in her life, save Art and Gretchen.

"Let's stop worrying about the unknown, shall we?" Gretchen tossed the spoon into the sink and held out two tubes of homemade icing Charlie had prepared. "Red or green?"

Charlie reluctantly acquiesced. "Green."

They began to decorate the cookie trees—for people this time. Earlier that morning, she and Rachel had scheduled the hot chocolate stand fund-raiser for that upcoming Wednesday evening, and they had a lot to do to prepare. The teens, now thankfully on an extended holiday break from school, were with Rachel at Paradise Paws, creating flyers on her computer to print and hang around town. Charlie and Gretchen had agreed not to tell the girls yet about the shelter being in trouble, thinking it best if they considered the fund-raiser an annual event to help with the upcoming new year. It wasn't a lie—just not the whole story.

And if things went well Wednesday, the teens wouldn't ever have to know the whole story.

Rachel had promised she'd call in a favor owed to her at the *Tulip Mound Press* and get a mention of the event in Wednesday's paper. Charlie was going to make the hot chocolate herself, and Gretchen had already promised to buy as many bags of mini marshmallows as she could find to contribute.

It was a short notice to pull this off, but she and Rachel agreed time was of the essence. They needed to start garnering attention for Paradise Paws's funding crisis *now*.

The rest was out of their hands.

Charlie took a quick peek at her watch before trimming the next cookie tree with icing. It was Monday, midafternoon. Blake had most likely already contacted Mr. Raines, if he'd taken her advice on how to sweet-talk Mrs. Hoffman. But she wasn't supposed to be worrying about that right now, was she?

Gretchen peered at her from the other side of the counter. "I know what you're thinking."

Of course she did. Charlie tossed back her ponytail. "I'm trying! Speaking of things we're not supposed to worry about…what happened with Nadia and Sabrina last night?" After Blake's confession, Charlie had called Gretchen as promised to make sure the house mom knew exactly what had gone down.

"We had a family meeting."

How Gretchen could keep her tone so calm over what had to have been an emotionally charged event would always beat Charlie. "And?" She piped a silver star on top of the next tree.

Gretchen carefully dotted her cookie with red ornament balls. "Art addressed the fight. Both girls confessed and apologized. Sabrina admitted she ultimately started it, and we had a long chat about jealousy and the best way to handle our feelings."

Charlie could almost guarantee most of the conversation went over Sabrina's head and that Nadia had rolled her eyes at least a dozen times, but maybe something had sunk in. All they could do was try—and remember that at the end of the day, despite how much ground it seemed they weren't gaining…these teens were so much better off than they'd be otherwise.

The same might not be able to be said about the shelter dogs after Blake's next meeting.

"And then both of them got extra chores to do—together." Gretchen winked. "I figured a little teamwork could go a long way."

"You're doing a great job." Charlie impulsively set down her tube of icing and hugged Gretchen.

The house mother returned the warm gesture, then pulled back to look pointedly into Charlie's eyes. "And so are you. Those girls talk to you about things they don't share with me. You're making a difference—and I love that you're officially a CASA volunteer now. You're going to help so many girls. You're already helping Tori feel like she belongs."

Charlie smiled and resumed piping. She truly hoped so. But if she couldn't save Paradise Paws and keep the teens from losing one of the few things in their lives they'd dared to get attached to, how much would it even matter?

The only B&B in Tulip Mound was thankfully not as floral in its decor as the town's namesake suggested.

Blake kicked his feet up on the front porch railing of the Hummingbird Inn and adjusted his laptop in his lap. Despite the surprisingly modern—and tulip-free—vibe of his room, he'd needed some fresh air, so he was taking full advantage of the afternoon sun warming the white wooden porch.

He'd finally gotten past Mrs. Hoffman, after making small talk about her three grandchildren and grandcat for a solid twenty-five minutes, and had been given that which was only awarded to those who were worthy—a direct appointment with Mr. Raines.

He felt like he'd managed to pull the sword from the stone or lift Thor's hammer, but even Blake's new superhero status couldn't account for one more unavoidable hiccup—Mr. Raines was out of town and wasn't available to meet until Thursday.

Blake saved and closed out the spreadsheet on his screen, his brain whirring as fast as the machine perched on his lap. Three more days. Could he wait that long? This kind of deal wasn't one to make on the phone with a stranger. On the other hand, he couldn't stay in Tulip Mound indefinitely, either.

Which led him to yet another problem—how was he going to be able to see Tori again in the meantime? And in a way that felt organic to her *and* to Gretchen and Charlie? He couldn't raise suspicion about his involvement yet—especially not after that whole incident with the tree.

He needed to figure something out, and fast. As it stood, after his last few interactions with Tori, he was probably registering on her radar more as someone she'd be glad to see leave town, rather than someone she'd ever consider leaving town with—biological family or not.

"Hey."

Blake jumped at the sudden voice sounding below him in the front yard. He sat upright and shut his laptop as Charlie climbed the porch stairs, wearing an oversize hoodie and an electric-blue wool headband that popped against her red hair.

Something green was smeared across one cheekbone, and he briefly debated telling her. Then he grinned. No rush. Besides, it wasn't fair for someone who considered him the enemy to look so incredibly beautiful in the middle of a Monday afternoon.

"I was going to apologize for showing up unexpectedly, but I remember that's how you apparently handle business, too." The wind rustled, sending a brisk chill across the porch and loose strands of Charlie's red hair dancing across her cheeks. She grinned.

Why had he never kissed her?

He shook his head to clear it. "No problem." He planted his feet on the ground—attempting to get his head out of the clouds—and stood, setting his computer on the chair behind him. "I'm assuming you're not here for a room."

She snorted. "As lovely as the Hummingbird is, I'm not." She hesitated, glancing everywhere but at him. No issue there—it gave him longer to admire the curve of her jaw and the nervous way she rolled in her bottom lip.

She finally met his gaze, and the vulnerability in her expression tripped up his stomach. "I came to ask you one more time to change your mind."

"About…"

She narrowed her eyes. "You know what."

He'd hoped it'd be anything else. Anything else he could give her. He let out a long breath. "Charlie…"

"I know." She held up both hands in defense. "It was a long shot."

More than long. He pointed at her. "You're stubborn."

She lifted her chin. "I prefer dedicated."

"Bullheaded." He took a step toward her.

"I believe you mean *tenacious*."

Two more steps closer. "Beautiful."

She visibly swallowed and backed up. "Um…"

"I figured that one would stump you." He pursued her across the porch, matching her steps until she hit the railing.

She gripped the wooden beam behind her with both hands. "You're not playing fair."

Neither was she, and she didn't even know it. She smelled like peppermint and cookie dough and everything else uniquely Charlie that he'd never been able to get out of his mind. "You smell like a Christmas candle."

She quirked an eyebrow at him. "I've been baking."

"As usual." He dared to move an inch closer. "You've got evidence on your cheek." Before he could lose his nerve or she could argue, he gently wiped it away with his finger.

Her eyes widened, then softened into something more like the Charlie he once knew. The one who fought for what she was passionate about but, at the end of a hard day, came to him for comfort. Now, he was the one she was fighting.

Then a vulnerable question of his own begged to be asked. "Do you ever wonder what if?"

She glanced down, then straight into his eyes. "Of course I do. You left, Blake. You *bailed*."

Frustration gnawed in his gut at her limited perspective. "You know it wasn't like that."

"Do I?" Challenge lit her fiery gaze.

"I didn't have a choice." She hadn't left him one. How could she not see that?

"We all have choices." She drew in a ragged breath.

"For example, you have the choice to stop this attempt to shut down Paradise Paws."

That's all she was going to care about. Charlie was a broken record when she fixed her sights on something.

He just wished she'd ever fixed them on him.

Blake deflated as he backed away from the railing—from her. From what could have been.

Charlie straightened, tugging down her sweater and then reaching up to pat her hair self-consciously. "Look, we decided to put together some fund-raisers for Paradise Paws and try to get the money raised to relocate the shelter if we have to. Starting with a hot chocolate stand on Wednesday."

"Sounds like a plan. I hope it goes well." He needed her to understand that he did care—more than she'd ever know—but she couldn't realize that right now. He refused to spill the beans about Tori, because if that timing was thrown off, it'd be detrimental to everyone involved.

He headed back to the porch chair and his computer, the heaviness of all the unknown weighing on his shoulders like a wet blanket. He had no idea what to do about developing a relationship with his niece. On top of that, the only woman whose opinion he'd ever truly valued currently thought he was the scum of the earth…and his job hinged on keeping her mad at him.

At this point, all he wanted for Christmas was to run away.

"Come to the hot chocolate stand."

He turned, and Charlie's eyes widened as if she couldn't believe she'd invited him, either. Then she charged on in full Charlie fashion, moving closer. "I mean, the least you can do is buy a cup of cocoa, right?"

"Is it your recipe?" Even as the words left his lips, he

could taste the rich chocolate Charlie had always used in her homemade cocoa. He wasn't sure of her secret ingredient, but every time he drank it, it'd left him feeling full and warm in more ways than one.

Or maybe that had just been her company.

She leaned one hip against the white railing. "Of course."

He squinted. "Marshmallows?" His mind demanded to know why she'd even invite him in the first place, while his heart demanded he hush and go with it. Maybe this was her olive branch after that truth bomb she'd dropped on him.

"Are these really your conditions?" She let out a part huff, part laugh. "Yes, there will be mini marshmallows. *And* peppermint stirring sticks."

"You had me at marshmallows." She'd actually had him the first day he'd seen her at Tulip Mound High— the new girl with flaming hair and a feisty personality to match. She'd fussed at the football team for littering in the schoolyard, always wore mismatched socks and had a way of standing up to some of the hardest teachers with a respect that got her what she wanted. He'd admired her from afar weeks before he'd found the nerve to talk to her. She'd instantly claimed him as her best friend, and he wouldn't have had it any other way.

"Great. So, you'll come?" She dipped her chin and looked up at him.

He'd been staring. Blake cleared his throat. "Sure. I can manage to buy a cup or two." He owed the shelter that much. And better yet, this would give him a chance to connect with Tori again. It'd be a win-win.

So why, after watching Charlie wave and head down the porch stairs, did he feel like he'd already lost?

Chapter Ten

It appeared that the hot chocolate stand was a success. Blake wove around several groups of jacket-clad people who stood in the yard of Paradise Paws, playing with the dogs, sipping cocoa and laughing as several younger children attempted to roll a snowman from the leftover icy sludge.

He made his way through the crowd toward the makeshift stand that'd been constructed a few yards from the shelter's entrance. Twinkle lights draped the wooden beams framing a short table, where a big thermos of cocoa stood ready for pouring. Tiny mason jars held a variety of toppings, while flyers featuring dogs currently up for adoption hung from another strand of Christmas lights via tiny clothespins. A large temporary pen had been constructed not far from the cocoa booth, where several of the resident dogs alternated strutting and barking for attention.

The entire scene looked like something from a movie setting. The only thing missing was fresh snowfall.

Blake nodded at Rachel, who operated the hot chocolate stand, as he stuffed a bill into a giant box covered with plaid wrapping paper. He recognized the big block letters reading Donations Appreciated as Charlie's handwriting—the same way she used to write on her school binders, with little circles on the stick of each letter.

"Thank you." Rachel's smile seemed warm enough, but then again, she wasn't the one with the personal vendetta against him. She swung her bulky plaid scarf out of her way and reached across the table. "Here you go."

He accepted the cup she held out. "Thank *you*. It smells amazing." He wanted to ask where Charlie was, but as much as he wanted to see her, he wanted to see Tori more. He couldn't handle another emotional back-and-forth with Charlie right now. He hadn't run into her since their encounter on the B&B porch a few afternoons prior, and maybe, for everyone's sake, it needed to stay that way.

Despite that fact, he was suddenly very eager to know what other quirks and preferences—like her handwriting—hadn't changed since high school. Did she still bite her lower lip when stumped on a math problem? Did she still absently twirl a pencil into her hair while concentrating, then have to untangle it afterward?

He'd probably never get to know. Blake bit back the rising disappointment and reached for the marshmallow scooper. Then a figure popped up from behind the table with a box of Styrofoam cups, and he jumped. Charlie.

"Hey." She looked as startled to see him as he was to see her.

"Hey."

They stared at each other—him gripping his cup, her gripping the box—long enough that Rachel politely cleared her throat.

He startled, attempting to stop noticing how brightly Charlie's eyes glowed next to her blue headband. "This is good." He held up his cocoa, accidentally sloshing a little over the side and onto his glove.

"You haven't drunk any yet." Rachel side-eyed him as she took the box of cups from Charlie's hands.

"Oh! Right." He went for the scooper, his hand shaking a little and accidentally scattering a dozen marshmallows onto the crunchy, frozen grass at his feet. "I was just about to add these."

"Here. I'll get it." Charlie took the spoon from him and dropped a generous amount into his cup, just the way he'd always liked it when she made it in high school. "The ground isn't hungry anymore." She winked.

He relaxed, grateful to see she didn't appear angry with him after their exchange Monday. "Thanks."

He finally took a sip, and for a wild moment, he wanted to tell her that he'd missed her. That it'd been so boring sitting around the B&B for several days by himself. He'd watched three Christmas movies and read an entire book. Tried to get ahead on some other projects at work. Read articles on how to parent a foster kid, then a dozen more on being a good stepfather. Technically, he was Tori's uncle, but the two dynamics seemed similar. Unfortunately, there wasn't a lot of information out there that covered his exact situation.

He wanted to tell Charlie all that. He wanted to know how her week was. What she was baking next. And he wanted to tell her she looked really good in blue.

But an angry teen voice suddenly sounded behind him before he could do any of that.

"Hey, look who it is—Benedict Arnold."

He turned to find Sabrina glaring at him, a cup of hot chocolate in her hand. Several marshmallows floated on top, dusted with red and green sprinkles. Her tone was decidedly *not* festive.

She lifted her chin. "Thanks for tattling. I had to do extra chores."

Behind the table, Rachel let out an amused snort.

Blake opened his mouth, then shut it, unsure how to respond. Sabrina had done something wrong and gotten in trouble for it—that wasn't Blake's fault. She had to own her mistake and her punishment.

But man, he felt bad for having inadvertently caused it.

Charlie came around the side of the booth and stood beside him, gently touching his forearm before shooting him a sideways glance. *Watch this*, she mouthed. "How do you know who Benedict Arnold is?" she asked Sabrina.

Sabrina shrugged as if she couldn't care less. "We learned about him in school last month."

"That's cool." Charlie widened her eyes slightly at Blake, as if suggesting he follow her lead. Then she turned back to Sabrina. "History can provide some pretty good insult material, huh?"

Surprise flicked across the teen's face, and she nodded slowly. "I guess."

He got it now. Blake tilted his head, thinking. "Have you learned about Shakespeare yet? He had some pretty good ones."

Sabrina studied him suspiciously, and he pressed on before he lost her attention. "I believe one of them might particularly appeal to you." He gestured around them. "'I do wish thou wert a dog, that I might love thee something.'"

Sabrina stared, then suddenly snorted back a laugh. "Shakespeare wrote that?"

"Indeed, he did." Blake toasted her with his hot chocolate. "Look it up."

"I might have to do that. I thought he wrote boring stuff." She narrowed her eyes at Blake, but this time thoughtfully rather than in anger. "Maybe you're not so bad." Then she flounced off into the crowd before he could respond.

Charlie slapped him a high five with her gloved hand before they began to walk away from the stand. "Nice."

"Thanks for the tip." His heart was racing like he'd survived an encounter with a dangerous animal. Was that how all parents of teens felt?

"You just have to know how to reach them." She shrugged. "I mean, ultimately, name-calling isn't much better than fighting, but if you can get them sharing funny insults that make them laugh, it usually forms a bond and the argument is over before it can fully begin. It's all about picking your battles."

He shook his head. "How do you know so much about teen girls?"

"Besides the fact that I was one?"

He tugged at the collar of his jacket. "Well, yeah. Obviously, that."

"I'm kidding. With teen girls, you have to play it by ear. We're all learning as we go." She pointed subtly over at the group of kids crowding around the dog pen. "I've *been* a teen girl, but this is my first time to ever influence one, and that's a whole different ball game, I assure you."

He followed her gaze. Tori tossed a marshmallow at Nadia, and it bounced off her braid. She immediately plucked one from her cup and returned fire, but Tori caught it proudly in her mouth. Then they both doubled over laughing.

He shook his head with a smile. "They're pretty great, though, huh?"

"They really are."

For the first time since arriving in Tulip Mound, he could envision being Tori's uncle. Watching her play with the other kids now, he could almost forget how many hard knocks she'd had. But then he remembered how his sister had lied about her very existence, and his stomach twisted with anger. Why hadn't she given him the chance to be involved if she didn't want to be? Had Danielle thought so poorly of him, or was it the substance abuse clouding her decisions all those years? Or, just as likely, their dad in her ear with more lies.

Regardless, the fact remained that Danielle had relinquished her parental rights long ago, and he didn't even know where she was. In prison again or not, she clearly didn't want anything to do with motherhood, and he owed it to Tori to take up the mantle. He couldn't be a mom, but he could be an amazing uncle if given the chance. A father figure of sorts, someone to provide for her and take care of her. He could be the dad that he'd never had, either. He and Tori had that much in common, at least.

But as he watched Charlie meander over to help Tori and Nadia hand out flyers, his heart sank. To be a father to Tori, he'd ultimately have to pull the girl from Tulip Mound and the home she'd made over the last several months. Would that do more harm than good? He was still a stranger to her.

Determination rose, and Blake quickly gulped down the rest of his cocoa. He'd just have to fix that, wouldn't he? Before he could make an effort to head their way, his cell rang.

"Mr. Bryant, it's Anita Duncan." Tori's caseworker's

voice filled his ear. "Just checking in on progress and letting you know I've scheduled you a meeting with Tori's CASA worker for Friday afternoon."

There was no getting around it this time. Anita was right—maybe the CASA volunteer would be able to help him navigate this new playing field he kept striking out on. He needed all the help he could get. And since he couldn't trust Charlie with his secret yet, he needed an advocate on the inside.

"Sounds great." He nodded, pushing back the lingering worry that attempted to crawl up his chest. "I'll be available anytime."

"It looks like you'll be meeting Ms. Bussey at the—" her voice trailed off, and papers shuffled "—Sweet Briar Café at 3:00 p.m."

"I'm sorry—*who*?" His throat knotted, and he stared across the yard at Charlie, who laughed as she played sword fight with Tori via a rolled-up flyer. Surely he'd heard wrong. Surely he'd just been watching her and thinking about her, so he thought he heard her name—

"Ms. Bussey. Her first name is Charlie." Anita's voice instantly warmed. "She'll be a great asset to you in this venture. Charlie is one of the most thorough and heartfelt volunteers we've ever had."

He didn't hear anything else Anita said as his hopes plummeted into the snow. His cold fingers tightened around the phone. Charlie would help him navigate, all right.

Navigate him all the way back to Colorado—and far away from Tori.

Charlie had no idea how much money had been shoved into the brightly decorated donation box, but she'd noticed Rachel periodically transferring the cash into a lockbox. That had to be a good sign, right?

Part of her regretted her decision to invite Blake. He'd donated earlier—she'd seen him put something inside the box when she'd been crouched down, digging for cups under the card table—but the price of him lingering in close proximity again might cost her more than she was willing to pay. His presence was starting to wreak havoc on her senses. That's why she'd stayed hidden behind the table for as long as possible, until her foot started to go numb.

She ran her finger around the rim of her cooling cocoa, hanging back as Blake strode across the yard toward Tori and Nadia, who were busily handing out flyers by the dog pen. He paused to sneeze twice into his elbow as he neared them, and she rolled her eyes with a reluctant smile. All these years, she'd had Blake filed away in a particular part of her mind—the part she allowed revisiting only periodically, usually with a box of chocolate and a sappy movie as accompaniment.

But now he was back. Live and in the flesh, stirring up just as many good memories as painful ones. It was a complicated mash-up.

"Here's your baby." Gretchen sidled up beside Charlie and passed over Cooper's leash. She'd volunteered to walk him around the grounds as an adoption advertisement while Charlie helped Rachel with the cocoa. "How are we doing?"

She loved that Gretchen referred to the fund-raising efforts as *we*. She'd had Charlie's back since the first day she moved into their home as a teenager. Despite everything else feeling so out of control right now, it was nice to know at least one thing wouldn't change.

"I haven't gotten a count yet, but the hot chocolate is flowing and the Christmas cookies we made are almost gone." She lifted one shoulder. "That's got to be a good sign."

"And the dogs?" Gretchen bent down to muss Cooper's dark beard. "This one was a hit with the crowd."

"I think Rachel's had two inquiries so far, both for Ranger." The gangly mutt had at least fifty percent Labrador retriever in him, which was a much easier sell. Still, it was a start. At least now the town had a fresh and much-needed reminder of what Paradise Paws did and its importance to the community.

"And Blake?" Gretchen met Charlie's eyes as she straightened.

"Blake? He's allergic. He's not adopting any." Charlie snorted.

"I meant, how *is* Blake?" Gretchen gently bumped Charlie's arm with her own, clad in a thick black jacket. She'd had that jacket for as long as Charlie could remember. Yet another thing reassuring and consistent about her foster mom.

"He's fine. I mean, I don't know."

"I saw you talking." Gretchen raised her eyebrows, her gaze gentle and expectant. And knowing. Always knowing.

How did she do that?

Charlie shifted Cooper's leash to her other hand. "We were just talking about the kids."

"He seems to have taken a real interest in the Tulip House girls." Gretchen nodded her head toward him standing by Tori and Nadia. Despite his occasional elbow sneeze, he and Nadia seemed to be having a running conversation. Tori lingered nearby, toeing the ground with her boot as she seemed to alternate listening to their conversation and squatting to pet Waffles inside the pen. "I think they remind him of you."

"You do?"

"Sure." Gretchen guided Charlie toward the pen as she talked. "You met Blake in high school when you were around Nadia's age. You were also new to living with us, adjusting to your first foster home that had no intentions of kicking you out."

"You mean, adjusting to a home of grace and forgiveness."

Gretchen wrapped her arm around Charlie's shoulders and squeezed. "I'm honored you label us that way."

"It's the truth." Charlie slowed her pace as they drew nearer to the pen. She didn't want Blake to hear this conversation. But it was one she needed to hear for herself. "You and Art…what you guys do at Tulip House now… it matters. I wouldn't be who I am today without you."

"And I can say the exact same for myself about you." Gretchen grasped Charlie's hand not holding the leash, her grip firm and sure. "You changed us for the better. You inspired the very creation of Tulip House."

Despite Gretchen and Art having made that clear to Charlie a dozen times over the years, she never tired of hearing it. It was as if each time the words washed over her, they sank in a little deeper and watered a different layer of her soul. "Speaking of the Tulip girls… I have a meeting tomorrow with a family member of Tori's that's stepped up and expressed interest. Has Anita called you yet?"

Gretchen nodded. "Just this morning. This is good news, right? You don't look particularly excited about it."

"It can be good. Or it could be a dead end. You know

how it goes." Charlie shrugged. "I never get my hopes up until I meet them—and I definitely won't mention it to Tori ahead of time. Too risky."

"Tori's blessed to have you as her CASA." Gretchen nodded. "You're a wise woman."

"Well, I learned from the best." Charlie nudged her.

"I'm glad you say that—because what I have to say next, I need you to hear and trust me." Gretchen's voice shifted to her firm tone, the one she used when doling out chores or talking to the teens about the importance of good morals. "Blake is *not* a bad guy."

"Well, he's not exactly a *good* guy." But even as the words left her mouth, she knew they were false. Charlie backpedaled as far as her bruised heart would allow. "I mean, he keeps saying he doesn't have a choice about negotiating this deal with Paradise Paws and Mr. Raines. And maybe that's true. But I don't think he's being fully honest about why he's here."

Or why he changed his name when he left. That one piece of the puzzle didn't fit any part of the frame around it, and it bugged her more than she wanted to admit.

"Everyone has secrets. That doesn't mean they're all diabolical." Gretchen tugged the leash free from Charlie's hand. "I'll watch this little one. Why don't you go talk to Blake?"

"And say what?" Charlie huffed back a laugh, crossing her now-empty arms over her stomach. She was shivering, but she didn't think it was from the December temps. "'Hey, Blake. Tell me something I don't know about you'?"

"That's one way to break the ice." Gretchen laughed and moved out of the way of a little boy running past them, wearing a puffy orange jacket and toting a sippy cup. A weary-looking woman chased after him, mur-

muring her apologies as she brushed past. "But I meant something more along the lines of genuine conversation. Besides, don't you know all you really need to about him by now?"

"I thought I did. But he's changed."

"Maybe not as much as you think." Gretchen smiled as she pulled Cooper in on his leash. "You know, all this has me reminiscing. I got your yearbook out earlier today. I'd almost forgotten you two were voted 'most likely to end up together' by your high school class."

"Don't remind me. Besides, Sarah Fairchild was voted 'most likely to become a movie star,' and last I heard she was a real estate agent in south Louisiana." Charlie glanced over at Blake, standing near the dog pen, and tried not to remember the person she'd spent so many formative years with. But the images lined up anyway, past and present, meshing into one man. One both old and new—and someone she really did want to get to know again.

If their circumstances were different, of course.

"Then maybe just pretend he's the exact same guy you knew at Thanksgiving eight years ago."

Gretchen's words twisted their way down into her stomach. Charlie swallowed hard against the memories as she watched Blake standing with Tori and Nadia. "Before or after he drove out of my life?"

Gretchen's response was interrupted by sudden raucous barking. Charlie turned just in time to see the orange-clad toddler smash through the pen, tumbling over the temporary planks and straight into the pile of dogs.

Chapter Eleven

"He was a hero." The stars in Sabrina's eyes shone almost as bright as the twinkle lights on the tree behind her. "He snatched that kid up like something from a movie."

He clearly had a new fan. Blake ran his hand down the length of his face. The whole experience at the fundraiser hadn't been nearly as exotic as Sabrina was making it sound, but at least she didn't seem to hate him anymore.

"We all saw it." Charlie's logical reminder didn't seem to stop Sabrina from replaying the entire event in vivid detail as they sat around Tulip House's Christmas tree.

Gretchen had insisted they come back there together for snacks after the commotion died down and Rachel and Charlie secured the dogs in the fenced backyard of Paradise Paws. Charlie sat by the fireplace next to Tori while Art lingered in the kitchen preparing some kind of comfort food, as he had described it. Nadia perched on the other end of the sofa by Blake, looking amused at Sabrina's dramatic retelling.

Sabrina pulled her legs up to her chest and wrapped her arms around them, grinning as she watched Blake as if Charlie had never spoken. "And then he handed the little boy over to his distraught mother…"

Charlie drummed her fingers on the knee of her jeans. "I wouldn't say she was *distraught*—"

"Oh, she was." Riley nodded from her position on the floor next to her sister. "Sabrina's not exaggerating. That part, anyway." She elbowed her.

Blake shifted uncomfortably on the couch. He wasn't a hero. He'd done what any responsible adult would have done in that situation—gotten the toddler away from the startled dogs before he could get trampled or bitten, checked him for injuries, and handed him over to his parent. Case closed. But apparently in Sabrina's eyes, he should be fitted for a red cape.

He was pretty sure the superheroes in the movies didn't have an allergic sneezing attack while saving the day, either. He sniffed.

"You hurt Waffles, though." Tori eyed him from the fireplace, most definitely not with the same adoration as Sabrina, and shook the snow globe she held in her hands.

"I know, and I'm sorry. I didn't mean to." Of all the dogs to step on while grabbing for the kid amid a falling fence and barking pile of canines, he'd somehow managed to find Tori's favorite. The long-eared pup was okay—Rachel had assured him of such after Tori's wails grew louder than the toddler's—but he'd felt awful watching the clunky dog squeal and limp away.

"Waffles is just fine. He was even walking normally by the time we left." Charlie wrapped her arm around Tori. "Blake didn't do it on purpose."

Charlie met Blake's eyes over Tori's head, and he nodded slightly, a lump forming in his throat. She had *no* idea how much defending him to Tori mattered. But he doubted she'd done it for him. More like Charlie's passion for truth and justice led her to speak out regardless of who benefited.

But it meant so much more than that to Blake.

He had to tell Charlie who he was before their CASA meeting Friday. But would that change the way she looked at him now? He felt like he was slowly—*painfully* slowly—making progress. No one had fully adjusted to his presence yet, and now he was about to rip the rug out from under them both.

Tori twisted around to look at Charlie for reassurance. "But what if it's not just a bruise? He's not adopted yet. Who's going to want him?"

Her voice pitched a little at the end of her question, and the real issue became obvious. She wasn't talking about Waffles anymore.

Riley and Sabrina fell silent, their expressions sober. Charlie ran her hand over Tori's hair, the gesture so natural and maternal, it made Blake's heart ache. Her innocent question tugged at the most guarded section of Blake's spirit, turning it immensely personal. *Who's going to want him?*

Who, indeed? Not his dad, after he'd disowned Blake. Nor his sister as she made her own selfish choices. And not Charlie, when he offered her what remained of his heart.

The pain of her rejection lapped fresh over him, like a rogue wave, and he shook his head to clear it. This wasn't about him. It was about Tori. And he wanted her, even if this wasn't quite the right time to tell her that.

He cleared his throat. "I'm sure Waffles will have a line of people wanting to adopt him after these fundraisers."

Tori stared into the little globe as fake snow cascaded around the cityscape. "But you don't know for sure."

No. He didn't. Blake felt Nadia's gaze boring into the side of his head as he scrambled for the right response.

Before he could find it, the teenager spoke up. "Tori, it wasn't Blake's fault. It was an accident."

He shot Nadia a thankful smile. At least the other kids were on his side now. But he'd never expected to bond with Sabrina and Nadia before Tori.

"I know." Tori's shoulders slumped. "It's just funny how accidents keep happening around here." She looked right at him as she spoke, but it wasn't with the same attitude Sabrina had used in the past. This expression was more sad than mad. The kid had a point. He *was* causing issues, first with the snowball, then with the tree and the fight, and now with her favorite dog.

What would Tori think when she realized who he was and why he was really in Tulip Mound? Talk about a double whammy. He was her uncle...and he was essentially shutting down Paradise Paws.

The lump in his throat grew several sizes, and he abruptly stood. "I'm going to see if Art and Gretchen need any help in the kitchen." Too bad he couldn't walk away from his own thoughts.

He hurried around the corner toward the kitchen, but a hand on his forearm brought him to a stop in the hallway. He turned. Charlie.

She dropped her hand as their gazes collided. "Are you okay?"

He hesitated, fighting the urge to tell her *everything*, right then and there. The whole truth. But he couldn't trust her. What if Charlie, in her own pain, told Tori too much too soon, or worse—nudged Tori away from him?

She wasn't just an influence over the girl as he once thought—she was her official CASA. She was legally committed to be in Tori's life and advocate for her in ways that he had never imagined.

He couldn't risk it, not until he knew Charlie had forgiven him and was on his side. He believed she wanted the best for Tori—but right now, he couldn't trust that she would see clearly what that looked like. Which basically meant he had until their official meeting tomorrow to hope she'd come to his side. There'd be no going back then.

An awfully familiar feeling filled his stomach as he looked down into Charlie's searching gaze—the same feeling he'd felt when they'd tripped over each other in the snow. And the same feeling he'd felt when he'd held his heart out to her eight years ago…one full of his least favorite emotion: vulnerability. There was only one solution.

Lie.

"I'm fine." He forced a smile, grateful she'd checked on him but hating that he couldn't be honest. "Just got a little stuffy in there."

The look in her eyes assured him she wasn't buying it. He should have known. He'd never been able to get away with anything with Charlie.

She crossed her arms over her purple sweater. "She loves hard."

"Tori?"

"Yeah. That's why she's upset about Waffles. On a logical level, she understands that obviously a child's safety comes before a dog's and that you did what you had to do." Charlie lowered her voice, glancing over her shoulder even though they were a room and a shut door away from the girls. "She just feels things deeper right now—she's searching, trying to figure out where she fits. Most teens pull away in this stage, but Tori is pressing in. She's testing what's secure."

His already drooping spirits sank lower, and he braced one shoulder against the hallway wall. It was as he feared. "And I'm failing that test."

"A little bit," Charlie agreed. She shifted her voice into a whisper, and his heart thudded. "But Blake—why are you even taking it?"

He looked beat-up—a far cry from the confident, surface-level-access-only Blake she'd run into last week at the college coffee shop. The last several days had clearly chipped away at him, revealing something soft under the hardened shell he'd shown up with. Tulip Mound had gotten to him. Tori apparently had, too.

Dare Charlie hope that she had, as well?

He cared about those teens in there, and she wasn't surprised. They had a way of sneaking into one's heart. But why the specific care for Tori? Was it just that she was the youngest, as he'd said about the Christmas tree? Her instincts said no. There was more to the story.

But she couldn't imagine why Corporate Blake from Colorado would care so much about a foster teen in his hometown.

As her court-appointed advocate, she needed to know Blake's answer.

She waited for him to respond, noting the way a new coat of dark stubble covered his jaw and the way the dimple in his cheek jumped, as if he were clenching his teeth. He stared back at her, with a look full of intention rather than procrastination—like he was debating something internally before he answered her question.

Standing this close to him in a dim hallway almost made her want to forget their past. Forget the way he'd abandoned her and never looked back. Though even if the past could disintegrate, the present loomed with fresh obstacles between them—namely, his involvement with Paradise Paws.

Yet standing in front of him now, Charlie found it hard to see a callous businessman with dire intentions. She could only see the Blake from eight years ago—the Blake whom Gretchen had encouraged her to see earlier that night. She blinked, but that Blake didn't go away.

Then something else caught her eye. Something green.

Mistletoe. Hanging right above the door frame heading into the kitchen.

Right above Blake's head.

The past and the present collided, and all her unspoken wishes and dreams propelled her forward. There was no logic. There was no single thought past that moment.

There were only her lips pressed against Blake's.

It was everything she'd ever imagined, and at the same time, nothing like it. He tasted like peppermint and smelled like evergreen. That permanent five o'clock shadow scrubbed gently against her chin, but she didn't care. She was kissing Blake. Her best friend. Her favorite memory. Her history.

Then reality crashed in, and she staggered backward a step. Her *history*.

"I'm sorry." She breathed out the word, unable to find any return air for herself. Everything in her seemed to float in the space between them, hovering, lingering, like flakes in a snow globe.

A space that Blake immediately filled.

Before she could protest or even decide she wanted

to, he pulled her into his arms, his lips firm yet gentle against hers. She gripped his shoulders for balance as the earth tilted and her head spun. They didn't speak—but Blake's kiss said more than he ever could have.

His arms held her steady, despite the spinning of everything she'd ever known. A dozen memories crowded for first place in her mind, a collage of the two of them from years ago.

She rose on her toes to kiss him deeper. The sudden movement propelled him backward a step, and he bumped into the closed kitchen door.

Just as it swung open.

They stumbled into the kitchen. Art caught Charlie's arm as Blake righted himself against the counter. "Sorry about that," Art said, wearing an oven mitt. Behind them, a timer dinged. "I thought someone had knocked."

Gretchen stared at them from across the island as Art moved to the oven, her eyes wide and her lips formed in a perfect O. A knowing grin crossed her expression. "I don't think they were knocking, dear."

"It's not like that." Charlie flushed, feeling the heat from her chest to the tips of her ears. She couldn't look any of them in the eye—she felt like a teenager getting busted with her boyfriend. Except she was an adult, and Blake wasn't her boyfriend. He never had been.

Which raised the question—what *was* he?

And what in the world had she just done?

Blake's face, surely not as red as hers but still pinker than usual, looked as if he were torn between beaming and breaking into a full-blown panic attack. His eyes darted from Charlie to Art to Gretchen, then back to Charlie. "We were coming to see if you needed any help."

"I think we've got it." Art turned from the stovetop,

where he'd just placed a baking sheet full of chocolate chip cookies. He'd used food coloring to turn the dough a mint green, like he did every Christmas.

The sight brought Charlie equal measures of relief and pain. Relief that she had someone consistent in her life… and pain that the person she wanted to fill that role had yet to prove it. One kiss in the hallway did not a commitment make. Blake would be leaving—again. It was only a matter of time. And the damage he left in his wake would reach far beyond a single kiss.

All their obstacles fell back into place, pushing through the mistletoe-dotted haze covering Charlie's heart and landing with the thud of reality.

She pushed up the sleeves of her sweatshirt, grabbed a spatula from the stand on the counter and motioned to Art. "I'll get these transferred to a plate." She needed something to do before she gave in to the press of tears crowding her eyes.

The atmosphere in the kitchen shifted, as if taking its cue from her stiff back. Art retreated from the stove, and she could sense him and Gretchen having a silent conversation behind her, like they'd always done when debating how to approach her over the years. Thankfully, they remained silent. If she spoke right now, she'd be done for.

With a thudding heart, she focused on scooping the cookies from the sheet as she tried to regain her composure. She wanted Blake to hug her. She wanted him to leave. She wanted to rewind the clock.

But the question was—which did she regret most? This kiss…or the fact that she hadn't kissed him eight years ago?

Blake cleared his throat. "It's getting late—and the girls have had a long night. I think I'm going to head back to the B&B." His tone indicated he had a rock-solid guard back up—not that she blamed him. She'd been the one to kiss him, out of nowhere, and now she was unable to even look at him. She wasn't being fair.

But if she opened the dam, the flood would never stop. She couldn't let that happen. Not while she was so confused inside.

Charlie took a deep breath and kept moving cookies onto the serving platter. "See you later," she chirped over her shoulder.

Gretchen's gentle tone followed Blake's heavy footsteps, then Charlie heard the opening and shutting of the back door. She sagged against the stove and pressed her fingers against her eyes as the tears demanded release.

He was gone a solid minute before she realized he'd never answered her question about Tori.

Chapter Twelve

Nothing was going as Blake expected. He hadn't expected to struggle to connect with Tori this badly, he hadn't expected Charlie to cross all borders of time and space and kiss him last night, and he definitely hadn't expected her to ignore him afterward.

Okay, maybe that part wasn't *as* surprising.

But sitting across the table from Mark Raines at the college coffee shop was downright shocking. He didn't know what he'd expected—a grandfatherly type, maybe, with a cowboy hat. Certainly, some form of an older man with money and a lot of heart in order to keep an animal rescue on his property for no profit.

He was *not* expecting a guy a little younger than himself, dressed in a crisp button-down shirt and pressed slacks, wearing wireless earbuds and carrying an iPad.

"You were probably expecting my father." Mark flashed a white smile as he leaned back in his wooden chair. "I might have mentioned I'm a junior."

"I'm sorry. Was it obvious?" Blake shook his head with a laugh, hope once more rising. It would have been a lot harder to talk an older man set in his ways into a deal

for Jitter Mugs. But this version of Mark Raines, whose
loafers looked more expensive than Blake's entire suit,
seemed to understand the concept of a win-win.

Blake's heart thumped. Make that a win-win for himself and Jitter Mugs. Not so much for the dogs—or for
Charlie and the girls at Tulip House.

"My father invested in a lot of properties over my lifetime, and now he's turning the business over to me. Mrs.
Hoffman helps me keep a lot of the time wasters away."
Mark toasted Blake with his paper coffee cup. "But I'm
always interested in hearing about a good opportunity."

Blake leaned forward. "And that's exactly what I
have." He felt himself switching into business mode, and
the automatic shift suddenly left him uncomfortable. He
couldn't get Charlie's betrayed face out of his mind—or
Waffles's, for that matter.

Mark raised his dark eyebrows as he took a sip of coffee, silently urging him on.

Blake hesitated. Then, he lifted his own cup full of the
latte the college kid behind the counter had prepared—
this time with hazelnut—and nodded. "But first, I'd love
to hear more about your father and your other properties."

He was stalling, going off script. If his boss saw him
now, he'd probably be out of a job. He could always blame
it on not knowing his audience, needing to get a feel
for the man before he knew which angle to approach to
work the desired deal. But deep down, all that would be
an excuse.

The bottom line was, until Blake could forget the
memory of Charlie's lips on his, he wasn't entirely sure
he wanted to make this deal in the first place.

His thoughts drifted as Mark droned on about the
other properties they had in the area. He nodded, but all

he could see was Charlie's beautiful brown eyes staring up into his. All he could hear was her soft breath as her lips whispered against his own.

And all he could feel was the abrupt chill that her absence had left behind as she pulled away.

Mark was still talking. Blake took a deep breath and tried to focus on what the man was saying.

"—expansion. Dad's always been a bit of a softy, to be honest. It looks great on the Christmas card and tax forms, if you know what I mean, but it doesn't pan out so great for the bottom line."

"And you're a bottom-line kind of guy." Blake recognized it now. Listening to him ramble—okay, half listening—had paid off. This young guy was obviously inexperienced, to have revealed what he did about his father. He wasn't just dressed for the part. He was taking over his father's investments with the same shark mentality Blake's own boss thrived on.

"Why waste money when you can make money?" Mark ripped open a packet of artificial sweetener and dumped it into his coffee.

"Why, indeed." Blake's voice trailed off and he thrummed his finger against the table, his thoughts racing to the backdrop of "Carol of the Bells" playing softly over the coffee shop speaker. This didn't feel right.

In fact, he could predict the next fifteen minutes to a T: he'd make the offer. Mark, in all his new-guy arrogance, would pretend it was too low. He'd throw out a counter—sale price. Blake would pretend to balk, though he already had permission to go a certain percentage over his initial offer and would rehash his points on why it was a good deal. They'd do that dance a few times while sipping subpar coffee and making surface-level small talk, until Mark finally caved and agreed to the initial offer.

Then Paradise Paws would have thirty days to relocate. Over the holidays.

While broke.

His timing couldn't be worse. Why couldn't all this have come down the pike in the springtime, instead of at Christmas? How in the world could he go through with this and pursue adopting Tori when she'd surely hate him? But how could he *not* make this offer and lose his job—and, therefore, any attempt at adopting Tori? No way would a judge move her from a group home to a family member who was an unemployed stranger.

"So, what do you have for me?" Mark's smile, while genuine enough, prompted he was ready to get down to business.

Blake took a long sip of his latte and breathed a silent prayer for guidance. If he truly believed God was sovereign and always on time, then he had to trust this was all happening for a reason and was not a cosmic mistake.

He set his cup down, opened his mouth—and his cell rang.

He pulled it from his pocket, grateful for the interruption. Then his eyes registered on the name and his heart skipped a beat.

Anita Duncan. Would the woman's calls ever stop shooting adrenaline straight through his veins? He held up one finger as he stood, chair legs screeching across the floor. "I'm so sorry, I've got to take this."

Mark nodded and reached for another sugar packet as Blake ducked his head and turned toward the back of the shop, where several shelves offered a colorful assortment of holiday-striped coffee mugs and packages of fresh ground beans. "Hello?"

"Mr. Bryant?" Her voice pinched. "We need to talk."

His spirits sagged as he stared at the row of snowflake-printed thermoses and desperately tried to remember his beliefs about God's timing.

Nadia pulled the plug from the wall, and the mixer abruptly stopped. "We've decided something."

Charlie scolded her with her eyes while reaching to plug the mixer back in. These were the days when taking the teens with her to bake while they were on holiday break wasn't always the most productive.

Then she remembered, as the mixer whirred back to life, that as disruptive as it often was, the girls were talking with her about their lives and feelings. And at the end of the day, that was more important than productivity—even if these treats *were* on a delivery deadline.

She pressed the off button. "What have you all decided?"

Nadia's eyes narrowed into a satisfied-canary expression as she leaned one hip against the community kitchen counter. Her dark, oversize sweater nearly swallowed her whole. "You and Blake would make a cute couple."

Charlie carefully schooled her features to try to keep the shock from showing. She lifted the beaters from the bowl of batter. "Unfortunately, cute isn't always the defining factor in matchmaking."

"But it sure helps." Sabrina swooped in, reaching over to swipe a lick of raw batter from the dripping beater. "Come on, admit it. You think he's good-looking."

She couldn't lie. She'd always taught the girls not to, and besides, it was obvious to anyone with a pulse that

Blake was attractive. They'd see through her if she tried to deny this universal truth. "Of course. But back to my original point—that's not always a defining factor in relationships."

She very intentionally did not let on that they had kissed the day before in the hallway. Nor did she let on that chemistry was at least *one* factor in a relationship, and that she and Blake had never lacked in that area. If anything, the spark she'd always felt toward him when they were younger and just friends had, indeed, morphed into a fire that threatened to alert Smokey Bear.

As much as she wished she knew what Blake was thinking after yesterday's kiss, she was equally grateful she hadn't heard from him. She needed time to process a few very hard facts—namely, he was leaving. And, more important, his task for why he was even here in the first place hadn't shifted. A dozen sprigs of mistletoe couldn't solve that problem.

She turned the mixer back on. Nothing had changed, and yet, it suddenly felt like everything had. She didn't know what to do with that, so—she baked. Besides, she'd need to have extra inventory for sale if they were going to move forward with another fund-raiser that weekend.

Suddenly, the mixer stopped. She looked up to see Tori holding the cord this time. "I don't know why you guys are saying *we*. I don't think Mr. Blake and Charlie would be good together at all."

"Because *we* do." Sabrina pointed to herself and Nadia. Riley had stayed at Tulip House with a headache, preferring to nap instead of bake. At the moment, Charlie sort of envied her. It had to be much more peaceful there.

Tori frowned, looking younger than her thirteen years

with the high ponytail Charlie insisted they wear when baking. "You guys are wrong. She's too good for him."

Charlie fought the smile threatening her face. "Now, girls…"

They ignored her vague warning. Sabrina crossed her arms over her chest as she squared off with Tori, cocking one jeans-clad hip. "Blake is a hero."

Well, that was a stretch of the truth, but—

Tori glared back. "No, he's not. He hurt me…*and* my dog."

"Waffles isn't your dog, Tori." Sabrina's know-it-all tone deflated Tori's anger, and the younger girl's shoulders drooped.

"Hey." Nadia's big-sister voice snapped between the two of them with all the effect of a firecracker. Both girls jumped. She pointed between them. "Knock it off." Her warning gaze lingered on Sabrina, expressing in no uncertain terms that she wouldn't take much more.

As much as Charlie loved seeing Nadia go into big-sister mode and defend Tori, she couldn't allow the older girl to keep getting into trouble. "Look, everyone needs to calm down. It doesn't matter who thinks what about me and Blake, anyway."

That ship had sailed. Okay, so maybe yesterday it'd eased back into the port for a minute, but not for long. It was way back out to sea now and, if history had anything to say about it, probably heading straight for a hurricane.

"It doesn't matter who thinks what except for you and Blake, you mean." Sabrina was back with her wry smile and waggly eyebrows. She leaned against the counter, her ponytail swishing across her shoulders. "I think he likes you, too."

"Too?" Charlie's eyes widened. Had the girls figured

out she still had lingering feelings for Blake? She'd tried
to be so careful around him. In fact, she'd even fooled
herself for a few days. But the truth was there, and after
last night, there was no more denying it. Which made no
sense.

He was the enemy.

Tori huffed, reaching over to swipe a finger against the
beater as Sabrina had. "Of course he likes her. Charlie is
sweet and pretty and great with animals. Why wouldn't he?"

"For once, we agree." Sabrina grudgingly nodded at
Tori.

"What's wrong with him?" Nadia ignored the other
two girls as they continued bantering with each other,
her gaze holding Charlie's steady. "You know he's handsome. He seems really nice. And he went out of his way
getting us all those Christmas trees. So, what gives?"

Sabrina and Tori were listening again now, the kitchen
silent except for the steady breathing of three eager teen
girls and the rhythmic ticking of the industrial clock
hanging on the wall over the sink.

She was going to have to tell them the truth. But
here—now? At Christmas? The whole story would certainly stop all this hero talk about Blake, but as much as
she wanted him to take the consequences for what he was
doing, something wouldn't let her. She still believed there
was more to the story. On top of that, until they knew if
the fund-raisers were going to work, she didn't want to
ruin the girls' holiday by predicting the imminent closure of Paradise Paws.

But maybe he wouldn't go through with the offer, after
all. Maybe he wouldn't meet with Mr. Raines and the
whole thing would go away. Then he'd...

Well, then he'd go back to Colorado and leave her with

nothing but a memory eight years in the making. But at least the dogs would be safe.

Not so much her heart.

She cleared her throat. "Like Mama Gretchen told you guys, Blake and I know each other from way back." Charlie chose her words carefully as she began to pour the batter into the bell-shaped molds. "We were best friends. It would be too weird."

But only because of his career and long-distance location. That kiss had been anything but weird. In fact, if she were the romantic sort, she'd relate it to something like finding the last jigsaw piece that had fallen on the floor and been lost for days after the completion of the puzzle. Even now, her chest fluttered and her lips tingled at the memory.

"So you're saying all this stuff he's been doing for us—the trees, coming to the fund-raiser, hanging out at Tulip House—that's all because he's just being a good friend to you?" Nadia's brow pitched with doubt.

"I don't know why he's doing it, to be honest." How *did* Blake feel about her? Had he been swept up in the moment like she had and immediately regretted the kiss afterward? Or had he been pursuing her all this past week and she'd been too blind to see it? She'd never know unless she asked. But asking would lead to an answer that she wasn't sure she was ready for.

Because at this point, no matter what he said in response—it would hurt.

Chapter Thirteen

He'd come to learn after these past few calls that Tori's caseworker was a very no-nonsense woman. Kind but firm, as Blake imagined she'd have to be to do her job well. She also seemed to want the best for Tori, which helped a lot.

Except for those days when Blake worried the best wasn't him.

Blake paced in front of the sinks in the men's room of the coffee shop, running his fingers through his hair while debating if he could shimmy out the back window and avoid Mark waiting for him out front. This was too much for one day, and he felt he'd reached the inevitable intersection point where, from here forward, no matter what he chose, every decision would result in dire consequences.

Anita had politely decreed it was time for him to make a solid decision. After his meeting tomorrow with Tori's CASA volunteer—with *Charlie*—Anita would be expecting him to call her and decide if he wanted to move forward with adoption proceedings and all the paperwork that entailed, or if he wanted to sign away his next-of-kin rights to Tori…which essentially meant he recognized their blood relation but chose to move on with his life. Without her.

Clearly that wasn't an option. But Blake had never imagined it would take this long for Tori to warm up to him. He'd tried to explain as much to Anita, and while she'd expressed sympathy, her hands were tied. The system couldn't stay in limbo indefinitely, and it wasn't fair to anyone to let it stay that way. He needed to figure this out, and the sooner the better.

"Dragging this out any longer will only hurt or confuse Tori" was the way she'd gently ended the conversation. He couldn't bear to tell Anita he still hadn't revealed his identity to Tori in the first place.

He braced his hands on the sides of the sink and stared in the mirror. Of course, it didn't help that he kept fumbling every move he made around the poor girl. He wouldn't want to go with him, either—not when she was starting to get established in school and had the other girls at Tulip House, and...

A sudden chilling thought struck him much harder and colder than any snowball. What if *that* was what was best for Tori? Staying at Tulip House, with Charlie and Art and Gretchen close by? What if it wasn't with him at all?

No one else in his family had wanted to keep in touch with him. Why should she? Like she'd clearly pointed out last night—he kept hurting her or hurting the things she cared about. Despite Nadia and even Sabrina starting to slowly come around to his presence, Tori kept a guard up. What if that was the Lord's way of telling him he'd misunderstood and was on the wrong path?

But if that was the case, why did he want to be a family so badly?

The bathroom door cracked open with a thud, and an

elderly man with a cane attempted to make his way inside. Blake rushed to hold the door for him, nodded at the man's thanks and glanced into the lobby. Mark still waited at their table, bent over his iPad while his foot tapped a rhythm under the table.

Another decision he had to make quickly.

Of course, there was one solution—a bad pitch. If he didn't make the offer sound good, Mark would refuse, and Blake could go back to his headquarters in Colorado and tell his boss that he'd tried, but he couldn't force someone into a sale. Then the dogs would stay safe, Charlie would stop hating him and he wouldn't be the bad guy anymore.

Except he'd be a liar. And his boss would send someone else, and Blake would still risk losing his job once the sale was easily made by a coworker. He needed the position for himself and Tori, even if that meant upsetting people in the short run. He had to play the long game—for Tori's sake.

He set his jaw and strode purposefully toward Mark's table. He'd pray first. But unless the Lord intervened, this sale would happen.

Time had run out.

Charlie pulled open the coffee shop door, juggling a box of newly baked gingerbread muffins in her other hand. The aroma of freshly ground beans wafted over her, and she took an appreciative sniff as she made her way inside.

She had dropped Tori, Nadia and Sabrina off at Paradise Paws after their baking session to start planning the next fund-raiser with Rachel. Nadia had shot her a questioning look over Tori's head as they piled out of her SUV. The older teen knew something was up—two spontaneous fund-raisers, back-to-back in one week? It was obvious Paradise Paws was struggling and needed help. Charlie wouldn't be able to keep that fact a secret, but she could at least keep Blake out of it awhile longer.

And maybe—just maybe—he would surprise her, and it wouldn't matter. Maybe he'd found a way to talk his company into pursuing a different property. Or maybe he'd canceled his meeting with Mark.

She almost hated to hope. But it was nearing Christmas, and if she'd ever allow herself the luxury, it was this month.

"Hey, Luke." She slid the box across the counter of the coffee bar as holiday music spilled out of the speakers overhead. The gangly college-aged barista wore a maroon apron over his casual clothes and, as usual, offered Charlie a big smile. As manager, he'd always been supportive of her start-up business. She'd been wondering lately if he didn't have some plans for his own.

"What have we got? The usual?" Luke picked up the package and started to peek inside, his blond hair sticking out in tufts from beneath the sides of his ball cap.

Charlie pushed up her long sleeves. "Gingerbread muffins, in honor of the season. I'm going to sell the rest of them I made today at the winter market this weekend."

"Nice." Luke nodded. "I'll be sure to stop by with my girlfriend. She loves those craft-fair thingies." He wrinkled his nose and shrugged. "And I like baked goods."

"Talk about an ideal match, right there." She laughed and tapped the box in front of Luke. "Let's mark these the same price that we usually do for the blueberry muffins and the scones. Oh, and can you grab me an extra bag? I want to save one for my meeting tomorrow afternoon."

"Got it." He quickly bagged a muffin and handed it to her, then grabbed a Magic Marker and scribbled the amount on the corner of the box. "I have a feeling these will sell like…well, like hotcakes. Ever thought of making those?"

"Holiday pancakes? Interesting. I might think on that." Charlie pulled her wallet from her bag and fumbled inside for cash. "Can you make me a latte?"

"On the house." He pushed away the dollar bills she extended. "Merry Christmas."

Man, she loved this town. She smiled. "Thanks, Luke." She tucked her wallet back into her purse, turning to observe the festive decorations. The baristas had gone all out with putting up a tree in the corner of the shop, covered in various coffee-themed ornaments. Mistletoe dangled over the double front doors adorned with giant wreaths tied with red bows.

Mistletoe reminded her of Blake, and her cheeks flooded with heat. She was going to have to address the kiss with him at some point. It was childish not to. But first, she had to figure out what in the world she was going to say. *That can never happen again. Please kiss me again. You're still leaving, right? Please don't leave.*

She groaned. Her jumbled thoughts were way too convoluted to risk leaving her lips. She had other things to think about, besides—like her upcoming CASA meeting the next afternoon regarding Tori.

It was incredibly hard to even think about Tori possibly leaving when she'd just gotten plugged in so well at Tulip House. But it was Charlie's job to be unbiased and support what was best for her assigned kid, and she'd do her job the way she was supposed to.

Her gaze flickered around the café until it landed on two men sitting at a table by the far window, and her breath hitched. Blake.

And Mark Raines Jr.

Her hopes scattered like a fresh dusting of snow. Blake hadn't canceled his meeting. She should have known better.

"Here you are!" Oblivious to her turmoil, Luke slid a cardboard sleeve onto her latte cup and handed it over the counter. "I added some peppermint sprinkles. Hope that's okay."

With shaky hands, she took the cup from him, unable to tear her gaze away from the men as they stood and continued talking, arms folded. She couldn't decipher the meaning behind Blake's neutral expression.

"Are you okay?" Luke's concern jerked her attention back to him. He frowned. "Should I have used the cinnamon sprinkles instead?"

"No, no, I'm sure this will be delicious." Charlie flashed him a half smile that probably looked as dead she felt inside. "Thank you so much." Then she looked back at Blake and Mark just as they broke into smiles and shook hands. Her stomach dropped somewhere down near her boots.

It was happening.

Paradise Paws had just received its official expiration date.

The Lord had intervened.

Blake shook Mark's hand as they stood, keeping a smile glued on his face that hopefully hid the surprise and weariness rushing through his body. Even though Blake hadn't held back on his sales pitch, Mark wanted time to mull it over. In all the scenarios Blake had imagined, that hadn't been one of them.

It looked like he'd be stuck in Tulip Mound a few more days. At least this way he'd have more time to try to make a better impression on Tori—assuming Charlie gave him a chance—but with this sale looming over his head, how would he concentrate? It'd take another divine intervention.

Blake nodded as Mark tucked his iPad into a leather case, lifted his hand in a wave and began to head toward the door. He turned last-minute, walking backward, and pointed at Blake. "I'll be in touch."

"Sounds good." Blake's tone sounded much more gracious than he felt, and for a moment, his legs felt shaky under him. He hadn't made the sale. Had his own subconscious held him back? Or had the Lord called his bluff and was telling Blake to slow down...to wait? Wasn't that what he'd prayed for before pitching to Mark?

Or maybe he wasn't that good at this anymore. Wasn't that what his boss kept hinting at lately? He didn't have the "killer instincts" he used to. Though, honestly, he didn't think he'd ever really had them. He'd started this whole career path in pure desperation to leave behind his roots and climb a ladder—any ladder at all—up, up and away from Tulip Mound.

And yet here he was, right back in the middle of his hometown and creating a bigger mess than before he left. Now, if he didn't make this deal happen, the career he'd worked the last near decade for would be on the line, and what would he do then?

He bit back a groan. He wasn't sure of anything at the moment, save for the dull pounding in his temples and the mild panic upping his heart rate a few beats per minute. His boss would be calling for an update later that night, and he had nothing positive to offer.

The speakers played a festive version of "Feliz Navidad," one that struck a stark contrast to his mood. He picked up his nearly empty coffee cup from the table, shouldered his bag and turned toward the front of the shop just as a small figure barreled toward him.

Charlie.

He stopped short just before running into her. "Oh! Hey." He shook his head to clear it, but the hurt in her deep brown eyes wasn't a trick of the light. *Well, back atcha.* He wasn't the one who had kissed her and practically run away.

"Was that it?" Charlie started to cross her arms, that defensive move she always made when trying to protect herself, then seemed to realize she held a cup of coffee. She took a sip instead, but the movement did little to hide her shaky hands. "Is it over?"

She was a spy. A beautiful spy, but still a spy. He frowned. "That was a *private* meeting."

She narrowed her eyes. "In a *public* space."

"What was I going to do, invite Mark to my room at the Hummingbird Inn for tea?" Blake ran his hand down his face. He didn't have time for Charlie's games, not with everything still unspoken between them. He sort of wanted to kiss her again. And he sort of wanted to walk…no, *run* after Mark to ask him to reconsider…yet on top of all that, he couldn't deny the generous measure of relief that, despite the pending consequences, this deal was currently out of his hands.

For a minute, he could stop being the bad guy.

Then the guardedness in her eyes shifted a little, revealing a vulnerable look he'd never been able to handle well with Charlie. It was the look that made him want to protect her, shelter her, buy her pieces of jewelry…specifically one for her left ring finger.

But he'd missed that chance years ago.

"Look, I didn't know you'd be meeting him here. I was

making a delivery." She drew a ragged breath. "But since you are here—is that it for Paradise Paws? Do I need to call Rachel and give her a heads-up?"

Blake studied the brave tilt of her chin, the barely contained anxiety in her eyes, the stubborn push of her shoulders, and his heart stammered. Was she really going to ignore the fact that she'd smacked a big one on him under the mistletoe yesterday and then never said another word?

He really didn't owe her an explanation about anything. This was a business deal that didn't concern her directly—indirectly, sure, but that wasn't and had never been his fault.

Of course, he *was* the one currently keeping a major secret from her about Tori. Guilt niggled, and he finally conceded. "Nothing is official yet."

Her stiff posture sagged. "Really?"

"Mark needs time to consider." He adjusted the bag strap on his shoulder. "Is there anything else?"

She opened her mouth, then closed it, shifting her coffee to her other hand. "Maybe we should talk."

Finally. If they'd ignored the elephant between them any longer, it would have needed a Santa hat. "I agree."

She moistened her lips with the tip of her tongue. His breath hitched, and he willed himself to stand still and not pull her into his arms. There wasn't any mistletoe today, but beyond that, he had to quit remembering what it'd been like to kiss her. Surely, she was going to express something along the same lines—the kiss had been a mistake.

Though his heart begged to differ.

She finally spoke. "The girls at Tulip House have decided to play matchmaker with us."

He paused. "Okay…"

"I just wanted you to be forewarned. Who knows what

they'll try next?" She laughed, avoiding his gaze. "Silly, huh? If they only knew."

Wait. "Knew our current dynamic? Or knew our history?" He tilted his head, unsure which answer he hoped she'd give. But it didn't really matter, did it? He wasn't foolish enough to believe he'd ever have another chance with Charlie, after all that stood between them. He was the bad guy. She'd made it abundantly clear.

And he was bound for a jet plane.

"Both." She focused on her coffee, rubbing her finger over the lid. She shrugged. "Either."

He might not ever have the liberty to kiss her again, but he couldn't handle going back to Colorado without her friendship. As much as being in her life with that kind of boundary would hurt, he'd take what he could get.

"Charlie…" He gently lifted her chin with one finger, then lowered his hand before he did something impulsive. "This doesn't have to be so awkward, you know."

She lifted one shoulder in a shrug. "I think it's better that way."

"Well, let the record show—I miss us. I miss your friendship."

"You sure didn't seem to have trouble walking away from it." She tossed back a big gulp of her drink, her eyes guarded.

He hitched his bag higher on his shoulder. "Mistakes were made."

"Yeah, well." Charlie took a step toward the door, a sad smile on her face. "The same could be said about yesterday."

This time, she left him standing behind, watching her go.

Chapter Fourteen

Friday morning, Blake decided it was time to up his game—on all accounts. He'd already checked Flour Power's social media page and discovered Charlie would be selling her baked goods all day at the annual downtown Tulip Mound Winter Market, so that meant he could kill two birds with one stone.

Figuratively, of course. The last thing he needed was for anyone to think he hated dogs *and* birds.

Blake strode up the sidewalk toward the giant blue banner stretched across Main Street, shoving his hands in his jacket pockets. The temperature had dipped, making him regret his decision not to wear gloves despite the bright midday sun shining overhead. He'd successfully dodged his boss's call last night and hadn't even had to try. He'd been in the shower at the time, and since his boss hadn't left a voice mail, he had no obligation to call back.

Of course, that meant now he was walking around on edge waiting for his cell to buzz in his pocket, but the longer he waited, the better chance he had of hearing from Mark Raines first.

He pressed through the growing crowd and headed toward the rows of booths offering handmade jewelry, custom art and cinnamon kettle corn. Blake sniffed the air appreciatively—someone had been frying turkey legs and funnel cake—before a red flyer taped to a lamppost caught his eye. He stopped beside a booth peddling candles to read it.

Paradise Paws Double the Fun-Draiser This Saturday! Let's Build a Snowman!

He paused. They were still at it—and Charlie hadn't invited him to this one. He kept reading, trying not to let that fact sting.

Enter Your Best Snowman to Win a Prize! Then Join Us Inside Tulip Mound's Community Kitchen to Thaw Out and Compete in an Epic Gingerbread House Contest.

Several rules in fine print, including the location and the nominal entry fee, accompanied the announcement, as did a handful of clip-art images of snowflakes. Blake kept walking slowly, nodding at the candlemaker as he passed but keeping his eye out for Charlie and her Flour Power booth. He hadn't heard how successful the first fundraiser had been, but his business radar sensed it hadn't been nearly enough to make a difference. How could it, selling cheap hot chocolate and relying mainly on donations? At best, they might have made enough to pay the bills for a month, but if Mark Raines said yes to Jitter Mugs's offer, that month would be all the shelter had left.

He moved out of the way of two kids in puffy jackets racing each other down the closed-off street, and for the first time, he thought about how conflicted Charlie must feel. They had chemistry together—undeniably—but she was in a difficult position. Just like he kept feeling torn between the urge to press in closer and the wisdom of backing away, she probably rode the same roller coaster of indecision.

Their past demanded closure, and yet here he was trying to pry open the door. Not to mention what she might think of him once she realized his connection to Tori. Keeping that secret had seemed so wise at first, but now he wondered. Was he being wise—or cowardly?

His steps slowed. Maybe coming to the market had been a bad idea.

But then the crowds parted, and there she was, red hair gleaming in the sun streaming into her open-sided booth. She wore a Flour Power logo apron tied over an emerald green sweater, and she smiled as she packaged up some baked goods for a young couple holding hands.

She looked like Christmas.

Like a magnet, Blake strode toward Charlie. Then he noticed Nadia and Tori standing slightly behind her, unboxing treats to refill the display case. He hung back a beat and smiled at the contented expression on Tori's face as she donned a pair of gloves and began arranging cookies on trays.

She looked so much like her mom, but in the innocent, youthful way he remembered Danielle as a kid. Then his smile faltered. She didn't deserve all this unknown in her life. Danielle, through selfish purposes, had actually given Tori a gift—a chance to grow up in an environment unaffected by substance abuse and various temptations.

But what if Tori took after her mom anyway? What if she refused to come live with Blake, or ended up in a home where she wasn't taught to beware of the addictive nature that ran in her family?

What if he couldn't save her?

He blinked, jerking back to the present. Charlie clearly hadn't seen him approach yet, as she called out after the departing customers, "Thanks again!" Then she turned and her eyes landed directly on Blake, her bright smile dimming slightly. "Oh, hey."

Blake swallowed, unable to shake the vulnerability his thoughts sent him spiraling toward. He wanted to tell Charlie so many things. Like how he was sorry for his part in what happened between them years ago, and that there was so much he'd never gotten to explain to her because he was young and stubborn and now it was most likely too late to matter. He wanted to tell her that she was the reason he'd never wanted a serious relationship since he left Tulip Mound. And that she was as pretty as she'd ever been and he'd do anything to be back in her good graces— to be her go-to friend again.

But he settled for saying what was currently acceptable—especially in front of the girls. "Hey."

Nadia shot him a genuine smile, while Tori lifted one gloved hand in a silent—and expressionless—wave. Apparently, nothing had changed there yet.

"What are you doing here?" Charlie's tone wasn't as rude as the words could have come across, but nonetheless, a rush of doubt filled him. He'd been so confident of his plan to win Tori's trust and Charlie's friendship back. But now, he wondered if he was just trying to force something that was clearly not meant to be—with both of them. He exhaled a silent prayer for wisdom.

"I came to shop." He gestured to Charlie's wares. "Rumor has it, you've got the best bakery in town."

Her cheeks flushed. "You know what they say about rumors."

"I think in this case they're true."

"They are," Nadia piped up from the back of the booth without looking up from her work.

Charlie dodged the compliment and held up a pair

of tongs, clicking them together twice in the air. "So, what'll it be?"

He stepped closer, studying the display case full of options, even though he'd rather study the smattering of freckles dotting Charlie's cheeks. Gingerbread muffins, iced cookies and cranberry scones filled several rows, while a separate, smaller case offered dog treats shaped like Santa hats and gingerbread men. "I'll take one muffin, two scones and four of those Santa hats."

"You realize those are for dogs, right?" She cast him a dubious look as she used the tongs to pull out a muffin and drop it into a paper sack.

"I know." Blake shrugged. "I figured I owed Waffles a few goodies."

Her expression softened, and she used a different pair of tongs to package the Santa hats. "That's really sweet."

He hoped Tori would agree. The younger girl glanced over, her face still unreadable, but at least she wasn't frowning at him anymore.

He took the two bags and handed over a twenty-dollar bill. "Keep the change."

"Thank you." Charlie slid the cash into a zippered bank bag and then, having nothing to do with her hands, crossed them awkwardly. They were back to that. "I hope you like them."

"You're assuming Waffles is going to share."

Nadia snorted. Tori's lips twitched, but she wasn't smiling yet.

Blake continued. "I saw the flyer for the next fund-raiser."

"Yeah, it's pretty last-minute, but I think it'll be fun." Charlie busied herself brushing crumbs from the white tablecloth. "The girls have worked hard with Rachel to brainstorm events and make the ads."

"I had the idea for the snowflake art." Tori shot him a

sidelong look as she began to rearrange the scones to fill
the space he'd left in the case.

"It was a great touch, Tor."

Finally, a smile. Then Nadia elbowed her, and they en-
gaged in a brief whispered conversation before their gazes
pinged between Charlie and Blake. Uh-oh.

Nadia sidled over closer to Charlie and beamed at him.
"You should come."

Charlie paused in her crumb scooping. "I don't think
that's really Blake's thing—"

"I'd love to," he interrupted before she could get any
further. He'd take any opportunity he could to mend
things with Tori—and Charlie, for that matter, though
both seemed like impossibly tall orders.

Tori's eyebrows rose in sync with Charlie's. "*You* want
to build a snowman?"

He shrugged. "Hey, I've been in Colorado for years.
You should see what I can do." More like, what the tal-
ented people in his neighborhood could do, but he'd
learned a few tricks from watching.

One corner of Charlie's lips turned up. "You realize
you can't wear a button-down and slacks for that activ-
ity, right?"

He was so happy she was relaxed and teasing, he didn't
even care that it was borderline making fun of him. "I'll
come prepared—I promise." He'd also come prepared to
donate, but no sense in pointing that out.

She resumed dusting crumbs. "And the gingerbread
house contest?"

"Yep. You're going down, Bussey." He was all bluff at
this point. Basically, unless hot glue guns were allowed,
he had a feeling his house wouldn't even be standing
upright by the time the judges came around. But banter
with Charlie was too much like the old days to resist.

Tori and Nadia shot each other a glance, and Nadia mouthed the words *told you so*. Blake frowned, then clarity struck. The matchmaking attempts. So *that's* why Nadia just invited him to the fund-raiser. They were trying to push them together, like Charlie had warned.

Charlie must have caught the attempt, too, because she pulled her keys from a purse tucked under the table and tossed them to Nadia. "Why don't you girls go check the back seat of my car? I'm pretty sure I left a box of dog treats under the passenger seat."

They obeyed, arguing over who was going to carry the keys as they walked off through the maze of booths.

"They're not very subtle, are they?" Blake laughed.

"About as subtle as a Rockefeller Center Christmas tree." Charlie adjusted her hair beneath her beanie as she glanced back at him. "Speaking of dramatic events—any word from Mark?"

And just like that, their easy banter ceased and the dangling anvil over them dropped another few inches. He pulled in a breath. "Not yet. I figure it'll be a few days."

She rolled in her lower lip. "Hopefully not too long."

He wasn't sure if she meant for anticipation's sake or for him going back to Colorado's sake. He didn't really want to confirm. "I truly hope the fund-raiser goes well."

She let out a slow sigh. "I know you do."

"Ah, so you finally accept I'm not actually a villain?" He raised his eyebrows.

A hint of a smile crossed her face. She pointed the tongs at him. "I wouldn't go that far."

He sobered. "All the best villains have their own backstory, you know."

"But this isn't the movies. There's no guaranteed happily-ever-after."

"Sometimes a script can be rewritten."

She shrugged, as if doubtful. He felt the same, to be honest. It would take more of that divine intervention to fix things between him and Charlie. So many years wasted—and so many secrets and obstacles still in the way. He'd never be a hero in her eyes—no matter how many dog treats he purchased or how many toddlers he rescued from collapsing fences. He needed to accept it and stop trying to read hope into places where there wasn't any.

He adjusted the two sacks in his hands, his heart pounding as he prepared to take another honest leap. He had to tell her about Tori. It had already been too long—now he would just look suspicious. It was time for the whole truth. Maybe Charlie could help him break the barrier between him and Tori once and for all. Her approval would go a long way—if he could keep it.

He drew a deep breath, all previous facades down. "Charlie, I really need to—"

Suddenly, a large family crowded the booth, two young girls pushing past him and clamoring over which cookie they wanted as their parents hollered instructions to not touch anything. The woman balanced a toddler on one hip while the father wrestled a diaper bag and wallet from the undercarriage of a plaid stroller. "Excuse us," the woman said as the kid in her arms accidentally kicked Blake in the ribs.

The Lord's intervention again? It was getting hard to tell.

"I better go deliver these to Waffles." He raised his voice and held up the bag of dog treats as he backed away and waved at Charlie. "See you at the contest, if not before."

It'd be before, all right. He checked his watch as he strode away from the table. It'd be in about four hours.

Chapter Fifteen

Tulip Mound residents officially considered breakfast a desirable option for any time of day, and Charlie was ready to do her citizenly duty with a plate full of pancakes. Standing at her booth all morning at the winter market had worked up her appetite, as had skipping lunch to sell as many baked goods as possible.

Hopefully Tori's family member wouldn't mind Charlie scarfing down a short stack while they chatted.

She paused inside the front door of the Sweet Briar Café, lifting one hand in a wave to Elisa Carrington standing behind the counter. The sweet thirtysomething owner of the café wore a red apron dusted with flour and grease, and her messy bun of blond curls seemed to be struggling to stay upright. She waved back with a pink-lipsticked grin. "Want me to start you a stack?"

Charlie nodded and held up three fingers to indicate how many she wanted. Then, as she looked around for the man she was meeting, she realized Anita had never told her what he looked like. Had she even given his name? She only remembered the woman saying "Tori's uncle." That didn't bode well for the caseworker's thoughts on how serious the man was about Tori, so maybe this meeting could be brief.

At least there'd be pancakes.

She stepped out of the doorway so another patron could leave, then scanned the restaurant, looking for a man sitting by himself. She recognized half the people there, crowding the booths. Mr. Dean and Mr. Dale, two elderly twin brothers, sat in their usual back corner booth, wearing matching buffalo-plaid shirts and arguing over a game of chess. The high school principal, Mrs. Crowder, was there as well, polishing off a plate of cinnamon rolls as she sat across from the town librarian, who kept stealing glances at the book in her lap as Mrs. Crowder talked.

No sign of the man she was supposed to meet. Maybe he'd stood her up, which worked great as far as she was concerned. That told her all she needed to know about someone potentially interested in involving himself in Tori's life. If they couldn't even make a meeting…

Then a waitress carrying a tray of burgers and fries walked past a booth to Charlie's left, and a man with dark hair, sitting facing her, looked up. Their eyes met.

Blake.

All traces of hunger vanished as multiple emotions roiled in her stomach—an odd mixture of giddiness and dismay at seeing him again so soon. Had she told Blake she'd be here this afternoon? She didn't think she had when they'd talked at the market earlier. It could be co-incidence—after all, it *was* Tulip Mound, not exactly a metropolis of eating options.

Then his lips spread into a pained grin, and something apologetic flashed in his eyes.

Wait a minute.

Her hand gripped the back of the booth next to her, and

she continued to stare as the impossible possibility fought for traction in her mind. Blake—related to Tori? But...

She cast a desperate glance around the café, but there were no other men sitting alone. No other contenders.

Then Blake was at her elbow, grasping her arm and leading her toward his booth, where coffee steamed in a chipped floral-print mug. "I can explain."

She plopped onto the bench seat opposite him, a roaring in her ears. "I really hope so."

He leaned forward, lowering his voice. "Thirteen-plus years ago, my sister was in jail. She had a baby, and I knew nothing about it until roughly two weeks ago."

Charlie blinked. "You're Tori's uncle."

"I am."

She reached over, grabbed his mug and took a fortifying sip of caffeine. Her initial rush of confusion cleared, but a dozen more questions surfaced inside. "I'm her CASA worker." She kept parroting facts, racing to catch up. "How long did you know that?"

"Just since Wednesday. Anita called me to tell me about this meeting, and she told me your name."

A heads-up would have been nice on her side, too. Of all the times for Anita to bypass a detail. Charlie shook her head. "So you're working with Anita...and you want to be in Tori's life." More lines connected. "*That's* why you've been trying to so hard to connect with her." She let out a long breath before reaching for his mug again.

Blake signaled the waitress for another coffee. "I'm glad you finally know. I almost told you a dozen times why I was really here, but..."

"But what?"

He spread his hands in silent explanation before confirming. "But Paradise Paws."

Charlie inhaled deeply. "That's not just a cover for being back in town?"

He shook his head, and they both sobered, looking down at the table as the waitress appeared with a second cup of coffee and Charlie's triple stack of pancakes.

"Here's the syrup," the server chirped brightly, oblivious to the thunderstorm forming over their booth. She handed the sticky container to Charlie and dropped a pile of napkins on the table. "Enjoy."

Feeling like she was on autopilot, Charlie steadily poured syrup over her lunch, watching the glossy brown liquid run in rivers over the perfectly formed pancakes. The shock was dissipating, leaving an unfortunately clear view of reality. Blake had come to town to meet Tori. But the work issue remained. He really was after Mark Raines's land and, subsequently, the animal shelter.

The syrup puddled onto the plate and nearly ran over before she jerked back to the present and lowered the container.

Blake watched, his lips twisted with sympathy. "I'm sorry."

"It's not your fault." She tilted her head as she backtracked. "Well, yeah, some of it is. You could have told me sooner. But it's not your fault you didn't even know you were an uncle." She picked up her fork, but her appetite had fled. "And I guess I can see why you'd be hesitant to tell me, after everything that's happened."

"I'm glad you understand." Relief crowded his face as he leaned back in the booth. "I need you on my side."

"I said I understand." She dropped her fork with a clatter. "I never said I was committing to choosing teams. I'm on Tori's team. And the shelter's team."

"They're not one and the same, though." Blake raked

one hand over his hair, a hint of aggravation replacing the previous expression of relief. "Can't you see that?"

She narrowed her eyes. "How can you *not* see that they *are*?"

They stared at each other over her dripping plate of syrup and pancakes.

"Refill?" their waitress asked, gesturing with a coffee carafe. Then she glanced between them and quickly walked away without waiting for an answer.

Charlie scooted her plate farther away, trying to get a grip on the panic rushing through her. "Blake, you know how important Paradise Paws is to Tori. If you're essentially the tool used to shut it down and disband the animals, how in the world do you think she's going to respond to that?"

"I know." His eyes beseeched her. "That's why I need you in my corner to help cushion this with her. I don't have a choice. If I don't make this deal happen, my job is at stake."

"Mark could say no. Then what?"

"Then it's out of my hands, and hopefully my boss will see that. But if the deal fails because I just call it off, that's an entirely different situation—one I'll pay for. I can't exactly get fired and expect to move forward with guardianship." He exhaled a short breath. "I came here to try to get to know Tori. I want to be in her life." His voice cracked. "We're all the family each other has."

Charlie closed her eyes, but the image of Blake pleading with her didn't fade. For a moment, her heart played tug-of-war with wanting to help her long-lost best friend and wanting to protect— Protect her heart. Protect the dogs. Protect Tori.

At some point, I have to do my part and then just trust God.

Rachel's earlier words about the rescue were so true. Charlie fought for her grip on her figurative rope, but it was slipping fast. Yet how could she trust Blake again with all this? It was too messy, too important. If Tori and Blake truly connected, what would happen next? Would he take her away? She swallowed against the lump forming in her throat. Would she lose the shelter and Tori, all at the same time?

And Blake, all over again?

You can't control it. So, trust the One who can. Gretchen's advice grabbed the rope next and pulled again, determining the winner. It wasn't about trusting Blake. It was about trusting the Lord.

She surrendered.

"Fine." Charlie opened her eyes in time to catch Blake's look of surprise. Well, that made two of them. She tucked her hair behind her ears and took a fortifying breath. "I'll help you with Tori."

"Thank you." Relief sank his shoulders. "You can't tell her who I am, though. Not yet."

Oh, brother. Charlie sighed. "*You* need to tell her—and soon."

Blake nodded. "I know. I just want it to be good news when she learns the truth."

"What did you mean by you're all the family you both have?"

"Let's take a walk. I'll tell you." Blake reached for his wallet, then stood and dropped a few bills on the only nonsticky surface remaining on the table.

It was too cold to walk far, so Blake led the way three blocks south to the Hummingbird Inn, toting Charlie's bag of leftover pancakes for her like one would carry a carrot on a stick. So far, she followed willingly.

They strode in silence, their footsteps finding a matching rhythm like they'd always done despite his generous height difference. When they reached the B&B porch, Blake held open the front door and ushered her inside, resisting the urge to graze the small of her back with his hand as she walked past into the foyer. They might have kissed a few nights ago, but it was clear from their previous conversation that boundaries had been drawn.

And with the conversation looming before them, he doubted they'd ever be erased.

They made their way into the festively decorated sitting room, where B&B owner Noah Montgomery stood before a roaring fire.

"Hey, just in time." The introverted man's dark hair fell over his forehead, and he pushed up the sleeves of his flannel shirt as he turned. "Come warm up."

"Thanks, man." Blake gestured for Charlie to take the chair closest to the flames, and he set her to-go box on the end table beside her. "I think the temp is dropping out there."

"The forecast looks perfect for the snowman contest." Noah dipped his head at Charlie. "I plan to enter—and win."

"Glad to hear it." She smiled back at him, and a quiver of jealousy slid across Blake's stomach. Not about Noah—just that Blake wondered what it was like to be on the receiving end of Charlie's smile, with no baggage. No trauma. No secrets.

The thought sobered him as he sank into the chair across from Charlie.

Noah must have taken the hint, for he made himself scarce, pausing only to remind them of the complimentary sugar cookies in the B&B kitchen.

The grandfather clock in the corner of the room steadily ticked, building the pressure in Blake's chest. Now to find a way to start. How did one ease into a past littered with land mines—

"Why did you change your last name?"

Boom. That was one way to begin.

Blake leaned forward, bracing his forearms on his knees. Charlie watched him, her twice-ignored pancakes beside her, as if they, too, were waiting for his response. He should have practiced. But a script wouldn't make the conversation any easier. If he owed Charlie anything right now, it was raw vulnerability. He'd let his pride stand between them long enough. "Maybe I should tell you a story."

She raised an eyebrow.

He took a ragged breath. "Once upon a time, a boy fell for a girl."

She pulled her lip in, and he pressed on before he could decipher her expression and lose his nerve.

"She was quirky and passionate and misunderstood." He grimaced. "Of course, she had a chip on her shoulder the size of—"

"I did *not*."

Now it was his turn to cast a brow at her. "Who said this story was about you?"

She snapped her mouth shut.

Conviction twinged. He offered a smile, one that felt both genuine and slightly defeated. "It is, of course."

Her eyes widened.

"She pulled the boy in until he couldn't imagine a life without her. He didn't know how to tell her that, because he was young and not the brightest when it came to relationships. He'd never seen a good one play out—until he watched the girl's foster parents. They showed him what real love looked like, and he wondered if he'd ever be worthy of having that."

The guarded shadow slipped from Charlie's face. Blake stared into the flickering fire and continued. "He never told the girl that he didn't have much of a family of his own, either. It was easier to be there for her than to admit his own dysfunction."

Charlie's voice dipped. "Blake—"

"His sister was in and out of prison. His father, whose anger issues and substance abuse only grew worse every year, didn't exactly provide a stable home environment." He inhaled deeply. "But being with the girl was like finding a new kind of family." He paused to meet her gaze. "The kind he wanted to keep."

Memories of his time with Charlie in those golden years surfaced, one by one, stealing his breath and his attention. The fire danced in the fireplace, reminding him of all the nights around a bonfire he and Charlie had shared. Roasting marshmallows. Pretending to stargaze so he could just actually gaze at her.

Now for the hard part. Nothing to lose now—hadn't he lost it already? He cracked his knuckles and kept on. "One night, the boy came home on holiday break from college and had a major fight with his dad about his sister. His father decided to disown him and move down south. The man didn't want to be a father anymore, and he threw enough whiskey bottles to prove it."

Those memories pressed, too, but he shoved them down, and kept talking around the lump in this throat. "So the boy fled to the girl and asked her to come away with him. To start a new adventure."

Recognition dawned, highlighted in Charlie's wide-eyed expression by the fireplace's glow. She clenched her fists in her lap. "And that night, the girl said no."

Blake nodded slowly, emotion clogging his eyes as he repeated the fateful words. "And the girl said no."

The clock in the sitting room continued to count the seconds, even though for Charlie, time had all but stopped. Her mind whirled, trying to make sense of Blake's story and reconcile it with her own memories from that time.

"I had no idea." She couldn't get the image of college-aged Blake out of her mind. She'd known he wasn't close to his family, since he rarely ever spoke of them and only wanted to be around Gretchen and Art—and her. But his dad's drinking, the anger issues…she never would have guessed his home life had been that bad.

Then another puzzle piece slid into place. "That's why you changed your name."

Blake nodded his confirmation. "Dad was done with me. I was stubborn and hurt and decided that was my way of taking control back—letting go of all the ties that bound us."

She realized she'd been trying to do the same all these years, but toward Blake. Stuffing down the memories, making light of their connection, as if it hadn't happened. As if it hadn't mattered. "Did it work?"

"I thought so, for a while." Blake shifted forward in the chair. "After you said no to coming with me, I went back to school and focused on starting my career. I even graduated early. It seemed my new identity helped me change gears. I thought I was putting the past behind me…but it just followed me around on a long leash."

She knew that feeling. But as she thought of her own history, and the histories of the girls at Tulip House and how often she'd urged them never to be ashamed, one truth rose to the surface. "We can't hide who we are."

"Or who we care about." Blake's gaze darted to hers before flicking back to the fire.

She pulled in a tight breath. He had cared about her, just as she did him. Did he still?

Then she exhaled. Did it even matter? The fact would change nothing about their past or their present—both of which inexplicably tied into the future they couldn't have.

He continued. "When I changed my name, I hurt Tori and didn't even know it. That was part of why it took Anita so long to find me in Colorado." He shook his head, regret lingering in his eyes. "It's my fault."

"You couldn't possibly have known." She didn't understand why she felt such an intense need to defend Blake to himself, but she did. "Don't blame yourself."

"What about the rest of it?" His gaze sought hers. "Why'd you say no, Charlie?"

She stood. "Because I had a life here! I couldn't just leave Tulip Mound on a whim when you asked me to. What were we going to do—get married while you finished school and then just start a new life together?"

"Yes." His tone never wavered; neither did his open, honest expression as he looked up at her.

Oh.

She swallowed, crossing her arms to protect herself. "I couldn't do that, Blake. We were best friends."

The blue of his eyes darkened, like an ocean after a hurricane as he stood to join her. "You know we were more."

"Never officially." She waved her hand through the air, as if searching for something to grasp. "You hadn't ever even kissed me, Blake. I had no idea what you were thinking…you just suddenly wanted me to move back to college with you and leave all my plans and dreams here." The flames danced beside them, mirroring the fire of indignation in her heart. "Leave my *family*—the only one I ever had."

"I wanted to be your family."

The grandfather clock punctuated his statement with five ticks before she garnered the courage to say what was true. She turned slightly, finding it easier to look at the flickering golden light than directly at him. "I was in school, too—on a local scholarship. You asked me to just walk away from all that." Part of her had wanted to. The other part knew no relationship could maintain such an irresponsible start. "It was selfish."

"I see that now." His shoulders slumped. "At the time, I was just trying to put what I'd lost back together in the only way I knew how."

She winced, easing back a step. "So I was a default? Better than no family at all?"

"I didn't say that." He stepped toward her, closing the distance. "I know I blew it back then. But I'd really like to be your friend now."

She pushed her hair back with her hands, a wave of dizziness washing over her. She wasn't sure of anything right now, except that they couldn't go back—and she saw no way forward.

"Look, I'll help you with Tori." Charlie lowered herself back to the chair. "I don't know what's best for her long term, but her getting to know you right now could only be a good thing. So I'll do that. But I can't promise anything more."

He sobered as he sank back to the chair again. "Because you can't trust me?"

"Because you *left* me, Blake. You thought I said no and rejected you all those years ago, but *you're* the one who ended our relationship by vanishing. You threw us away."

The sting of it all washed afresh, and she shivered, everything in her going cold, despite the fire roaring beside her. The unread texts, the unanswered phone calls that eventually led to a "no longer in service" message. The closing of his social media accounts. The lack of hits in online address-record searches.

"You left me." She sounded like a record on repeat, but she couldn't bear to say the aching words still begging release. *Like everyone always does.* "And you're leaving again."

Chapter Sixteen

"Hey." Nadia tapped Tori's shoulder with her gloved hand before glancing around the snow-covered park. "Have you noticed how sad Mr. Bryant looks?"

"Yeah. I think they got into a fight." Tori bent and rummaged through a tote bag at their feet.

"You think?"

Tori nodded with authority as she stood, wielding a mini gardening hoe. "Totally. His shoulders have been slumped for, like, the last two days straight."

Shaking his head, Blake approached Nadia and Tori's hushed conversation—they were *really* bad at whispering—and waited a beat behind a snowman wearing a top hat as the girls attempted to roll snow into a large ball.

The fund-raiser event had started about an hour earlier, and already a variety of snowmen—and snowwomen—wearing scarves, beanies and gloves dotted the park adjacent to the community kitchen. A generous crowd milled about, forming their icy creations and taking breaks by the patio heaters set up in the parking lot. Charlie and Rachel had put a table near one of the giant heating lamps, taking entry fees and donations while Gretchen and Art peddled baked goods from Flour Power. But would it be enough to help Paradise Paws?

Speaking of—no matter how many times he checked his phone, Blake had yet to hear back from Mark Raines. He'd have to call later that evening and nudge, though he hated to do so. It put him in a position of need—and showing neediness while brokering a deal took away his power. Though right now, Mark had all of it, and they both knew it.

If only the guy realized exactly what was at stake.

Meanwhile, he had this to deal with. Blake stepped out from his hiding place as Tori and Nadia positioned their newest snowball on top of their lumpy start. "Your base is crooked."

The girls jumped, knocking their haphazardly formed ball into a pile of slushy snow at their booted feet. They shot each other guilty looks. "How long have you been standing there?" Tori asked, nervously swinging the gardening hoe.

"Not long." Blake knelt and began scooping snow into a more proportionate shape. "Definitely not long enough to be sad."

They glanced at each other again. "He heard us," Tori confirmed.

Nadia tossed her braid over the shoulder of her red jacket. "Well, you *are* sad, and I think it's because of you and Charlie. What'd you do?"

He kept packing snow. "I don't know what you're talking about."

Nadia snorted. "Come on, we're teenagers, not toddlers. We can tell you like her."

Like her. The innocent word choice felt like the world's greatest understatement, and yet, at the same time…

Blake looked across the little park at Charlie, standing by her table, smiling as she interacted with the community. Yes, he liked her. He always had, and he knew no matter what happened, he always would. But friends would be all they could ever be at this point, and Charlie didn't even seem open to that.

"*Like* like her," Tori added, in case there was any confusion.

Blake's gaze darted between them, and he realized— as he was starting to do a lot with these teenagers—that arguing was futile. "You're right, I do like her,"

Tori bent to help him with the snow, packing it with her shovel. "I think she likes you, too."

Maybe once upon a time. "Adult relationships get complicated."

"Only if you let them," Nadia countered.

"It's not that easy, trust me." Why was he going in circles with these two? "Right now, I just want to be her friend again." He finished making the smaller ball. "Help me with this one, will you?"

The three of them carefully lifted the second layer and secured it on top of the new base. "That's a lot better," Tori announced, clapping snow off her fuzzy mittens. "Now we just need a little one."

"What we *need* is a plan." Nadia crossed her slim arms around her middle and tilted her head at Blake. "What are you doing to do to win back her friendship?"

Back? He never had her in the first place. "I don't know that there's anything to do."

"You could kiss her again." Tori blurted the words, then immediately covered her face with her gloves. "Oops."

"Again?" Blake narrowed his eyes at them.

Nadia shouldered Tori with a gentle nudge. "That was a secret."

"How did you two— Never mind." These girls were sneaky, as he already knew from busting them eavesdropping at Tulip House. "No one is going to kiss again, trust me." He reached out and patted a lump smooth in the half-formed snowman.

Nadia pointed at him. "You must have messed up pretty badly in the past, huh?"

"Hey now. Why is everything automatically my fault?" He squared off with them.

"Well, was it?"

He squinted. "Sort of."

Nadia gestured with her gloved hands, as if to indicate her point.

"Why do adults make this stuff so hard? At my school, people just pass notes to tell someone they like them. Or get a friend to do it if they're shy." Tori shrugged as she stuck a stick into the snowman's side. "Do you want us to tell her?"

"No! I mean, no, thank you." The last thing he needed was Charlie thinking he was using Tori to get to her. Even though on that note, he'd asked Charlie to help him connect with Tori. Now, ironically, he and Tori were connecting on their own—over a conversation *about* Charlie.

He shook his head. "I broke Charlie's trust a long time ago, and I need to earn it back." At this point, all he could hope for was that she'd feel differently about giving their friendship another chance, after having time to process everything they'd discussed yesterday.

Though he had no idea how much longer he was going to be there to even give her a chance to do so. He automatically checked his phone messages again. Nothing from Mark.

"Maybe you need a big gesture—like in the movies." Nadia's voice pitched with excitement. "What if you got her an awesome Christmas gift?"

Christmas. That was next week, wasn't it? Maybe he should plan to stay through the holiday, even if the sale went through sooner. He should stick around, for Tori's sake. But despite their good banter today, would his niece want him there after she learned the truth about him—and his role with the dog shelter?

Tori pulled off her glove and hung it on the snowman's stick arm, then her eyes widened. She stepped back and surveyed their work in progress. "I just had an idea of something you could do for Charlie."

Nadia twisted her lips. "This should be good."

"Hear me out." Tori focused on Blake as excitement lit her gaze. For a moment, she looked just like Danielle again. Better yet, her eyes held zero resentment, wariness or concern. That was a first for him and Tori, and right now, she could probably ask him to jump into a tub of ice water and he would if it would make her happy.

She glanced over her shoulder, cupped her hands around her mouth and whispered her idea.

Once again, Charlie had been too busy to stop and gauge how successful the fund-raiser was. But from the steady flow of entry fees and donations and the sale of her baked goods—she was donating fifty percent of everything sold to Paradise Paws—it had to be decent. At one point, while she'd been helping Gretchen restock the display case with peanut butter Santa hats, Nadia had run up and asked for her car keys. Charlie hadn't even been able to ask why before the girl had taken them, thanked her and run off.

She really should find her and get them back. Plus, that would give her a good excuse to walk around and check out all the snowmen. Several local businesspeople had volunteered to be judges for both events, including Elisa from the Sweet Briar Café, Principal Crowder, Noah from the Hummingbird Inn, and Lulu, the owner of Oopsy Daisy Donuts.

"Go check it out. We'll hold down the fort." Gretchen waved her off as she took a bite of the spiced-apple scone Art held in front of her face. She grinned up at him, mouth covered in crumbs, and kissed him on the cheek.

Charlie turned away from the familiar display of affection, one she'd seen lived out in front of her since she was nearly fifteen years old. Gretchen and Art had something special—something she'd once imagined herself having with Blake. But now it was hard enough to muster up the courage to be a friend again. Was it because of her trust issues?

Or was it because, deep down, she knew she wouldn't ever be content to only be his friend?

She grabbed Cooper's leash from where he'd been secured near her table all afternoon and headed across the park. She didn't intend to hold a grudge against Blake— his explanation had cleared up a lot of assumptions she'd carried over the years. But it didn't change the fact that he was still a threat to the two things she loved most—Tori and the animal shelter. In one fell swoop, he was going to take both of those away.

She'd confided in Gretchen earlier that morning about Blake's big news—that *he* was the family member interested in taking Tori away. Gretchen had reacted as

Charlie wished she had been able to when Blake told her—surprise, followed immediately with grace, charm and buckets of trust in God.

Right now, the only thing Charlie could trust was the fact that nothing felt stable or secure—and might not again for a long time.

She tried to shake off her heavy mood, attempting to appreciate the Christmas carols blaring from a portable speaker as she and Cooper wove their way around the park, checking out the elaborate snowpeople crowding the square. Each entry had a label written in the snow before it. They passed Farmer Ice, who sported a carrot nose and a Brussels sprout smile; Ice, Ice Baby, who had a purple satin jacket draped around his back and a microphone taped to his twig arm; and Mama Snow, who carried an empty Starbucks cup and was surrounded by eight tiny snow children.

Still no sign of Tori, Nadia—or her keys.

"Charlie! Over here!"

She turned to see Nadia and Tori waving from a few stations over. Charlie tugged Cooper's leash in their direction. "Hey, girls. Where's your snowman?"

"Right here!" Tori stepped back alongside Nadia and gestured wildly to two snowpeople standing side by side. One wore sunglasses and a loosely draped tie and sported a scruffy five o'clock shadow made from what appeared to be crushed coal. The other figure was a girl, wearing a mop wig and an apron and holding a dog's leash. At the end of the leash was a snowcanine the size of Cooper, wearing a dog sweater with a peanut butter Santa hat perched on his icy head.

Charlie's eyes widened. Not *an* apron—her *favorite* apron, with the chocolate chip cookie design…the one that had been in her back seat just that morning. And that wasn't *a* dog sweater—it was Cooper's sweater with the Christmas tree on the back.

This snow figure was supposed to be her. And Cooper. And…

"What do you think?" Blake stepped up beside her, a tentative smile on his face.

Blake.

Her heart stammered at his sudden proximity, and her mind raced. She blinked at all three of them, automatically pulling Cooper back as he curiously sniffed his replica. "How did you—"

Nadia held up her car keys, jangling them as she wiggled her eyebrows and grinned. *Ah.* That was how. Her stomach flipped, and she wasn't sure how to respond.

Then Charlie's gaze registered the title etched in the snow before the elaborate group.

Voted Most Likely to End Up Together.

Chapter Seventeen

"It was our fault." Nadia's guilt-stricken face matched Tori's as they perched on two wooden chairs across from Charlie at Tulip House later that evening. Gretchen was in the living room finishing a Christmas movie with Riley and Sabrina, under oath not to come into the dining room while Charlie and the other girls wrapped gifts.

"So you keep saying." Charlie secured a folded corner of wrapping paper with a piece of tape, then flipped the box to do the same to the other side. She hoped Gretchen would like the plush new robe she'd gotten her. She hoped the girls would change the subject soon from the record-on-repeat one they had going.

And she really hoped she would be able to hide the myriad emotions flickering through her stomach the next time she saw Blake.

"I just feel bad." Nadia jerked her head in Tori's direction. "*We* feel bad."

"Yeah, we had the idea for the snowpeople to be you guys, but Blake didn't know we were going to write that in the snow afterward. He didn't see it until you did." Tori rolled in her lower lip, twirling a piece of spare ribbon around her finger. "We just thought maybe you needed a gesture. I remembered seeing that title for you two in your old yearbook that Mama Gretchen left out, and—"

"Ah, so that's how you guys knew." Charlie looked up, tape dangling off one finger. Forever sneaky. But she still had one question. "But why did you think I needed a gesture?"

After she'd seen the inscription, she'd made an excuse about needing to get back to the ticket booth and her baked goods and hauled Cooper away before Blake could speak another word.

Tori twirled the ribbon fast. "A gesture to make you not be upset at Blake anymore."

"Yeah, it seemed like whatever happened with you guys was in the past." Nadia shrugged, running her fingers through the ends of her long braid that she'd tugged over her shoulder. "And he seems cool. So I don't get it."

Charlie taped the final corner of the paper and then set the glitter-dusted gift for Gretchen aside. She let out a slow sigh. "Girls, the matchmaking effort is sweet. I appreciate that you care about me. But it's also dangerous. You don't know our history. Meddling with adult relationships can be kind of disastrous." To put it mildly.

"But he just wants to be your friend again." Tori's protest tweaked Charlie's heart. She was supposed to be helping Blake connect with Tori, so she couldn't explain how badly Blake had hurt her in the past without potentially stirring up Tori's loyalties and driving a wedge between her and Blake right when it mattered most.

Though, in hindsight, maybe she'd been too hard on him at the fund-raiser, jetting off so quickly with Cooper. Especially if he hadn't known the girls were going to write the inscription in the snow. At the time, she'd believed he'd been trying to matchmake himself—and bringing the girls into it. She should have known it'd been the other way around. Once again with Blake, she'd had a knee-jerk reaction and jumped to conclusions.

Would she ever be able to trust him?

It didn't matter. "The bottom line is, he's leaving soon." And Charlie had no idea what that would mean for Tori. Blake *had* to tell the younger girl the truth about being her uncle as quickly as possible. Christmas was rapidly approaching, and what then? Charlie also had no idea how long it would take for him to be granted guardianship—or if Tori would want it. If it came down to a debate in court, Charlie's voice as CASA would be strongly considered. Which meant she might be in a position to help decide whether Tori stayed in Tulip Mound... or moved away for good.

Talk about a rock and a hard place.

"You know what?" Charlie gathered the tape and scissors and began cleaning up the scraps of paper from the tabletop. "I think this conversation is way too heavy for this close to Christmas. I vote hot chocolate instead."

Tori's eyes lit up. "I second that vote."

Nadia was already moving to the refrigerator. "I've got the milk!"

As the girls began the routine of preparing their favorite holiday drink, Charlie tried to slip into the same festive spirit. It was almost Christmas.

But the only countdown she could really see was Blake's imminent departure from Tulip Mound.

It was finally Christmas Eve afternoon, and it was getting harder for Blake to deny reality. In less than forty-eight hours, the wonder of the holiday would be over, and he would be facing a very lonely plane ride back to Colorado. On top of that, he still hadn't heard from Mark on a final decision for the shelter, despite multiple messages left with Mrs. Hoffman. On the one hand, it made putting off the inevitable much easier to do. But on the other hand, it left quite a few things up in the air—namely, his job. At some point, he had to label Mark's lack of answer an answer and react accordingly.

After which he very likely might get fired.

Blake tugged the zipper along his mostly packed suitcase until it finally shut. He'd left out just enough clothes to cover the next day—Christmas—and something to wear on his return flight to Colorado on the twenty-sixth. Despite all the unknowns about his job, about Charlie and about the future, one thing was certain—it was time to tell Tori the truth about being her uncle. She seemed to have softened toward him this past week—largely because of Charlie's stamp of approval. Despite the lingering awkwardness between them since the fund-raiser, Charlie had gone out of her way to provide opportunities for him to connect with Tori—inviting him caroling with Gretchen, Art and the rest of the community; tagging along to see Santa; and helping deliver her last batch of baked goods before the holiday weekend started.

Apparently, Charlie had been caught up in her own denial of reality, because she hadn't brought up the dog shelter or Mark once in the past several days. Maybe she'd been trying to focus on Tori as well or was attempting to stay positive at Christmas. The unspoken giant obstacle between them seemed to shut down any further connection, though she had apologized for assuming the wrong motives behind the snowpeople creation. He hadn't given up on trying to be her friend—it was the least he could do after all she'd done for him and Tori. He finally felt like he was making progress with his secret niece—until the guilt over his job crept back in and put a damper on it all.

It'd be way too soon to take Tori with him on this flight home, legally, but after they talked, he'd hoped to at least arrive back in Denver with a solid plan to start the process—and bring her back with him for good on his next trip.

He eyed his suitcase as a dozen conflicting emotions raced through him, until one fact rose to the surface over the rest of the internal noise.

He didn't want to leave.

A knock sounded on the closed door of his room at the Hummingbird. Grateful for the distraction—and grateful that a knock was usually Noah announcing some kind of free food in the dining room—Blake strode to the door and opened it wide.

Not Noah. Charlie.

She blinked at him, her red hair loose and wild and spilling over the shoulders of her long black sweater. "Hey."

"Hey." He leaned one arm against the door frame, trying to hide his surprise.

"I was going to call, but I was passing by on my way home from the community kitchen and thought I'd stop by."

She wanted to talk. He started to invite her in, then realized he should probably step out, instead. He eased into the hallway, tucking the door shut behind him but not before she got a glimpse of his room. And his suitcase.

She swallowed visibly, then lifted her chin.

"I came to ask about Tori. You've got to tell her before you leave." She hesitated. "Unless you've decided not to go through with the adoption?"

Was that what she hoped for? He shifted in the doorway. "I wanted to tell her today, actually." He drew a deep breath. "I was hoping you could help me plan it."

"So you *are* intending on going through with it." Charlie's eyes didn't hold the joy he'd assumed they would at the thought of Tori being reunited with family.

"As long as Tori wants to. Anita said because of her age, she has a voice in the system, though the judge has the final decision." He crossed his arms over his chest, partly in defense—and partly to resist the urge to pull Charlie into a hug. She looked like she needed one, and he definitely did. "Of course, a good word from her CASA volunteer would go a long way."

Charlie nodded, but her eyes still seemed distant even as she smiled up at him. "Of course."

"Okay. I'll talk to her today, then." They made plans to meet at the Sweet Briar Café that afternoon for a snack.

It was settled. But nothing between them felt settled at all.

His heart sank as he shut the door and leaned against it, staring at the packed suitcase that seemed to symbolize everything that was wrong. As much as his heart felt led toward Tulip Mound, he had no idea at this point how to make it happen. If he stayed, where would he work? His lucrative life was built in Denver. He couldn't adopt a teenager after walking away from a solid career. And without a plan, he knew better than to even hint about his desire to stay to Charlie or Tori.

Charlie sat on the couch in the living room, admiring the fully decorated tree as Nadia, Tori, Sabrina and Riley crunched candy canes and squabbled over a game of UNO. In the background, the old cartoon version of the

Grinch played on the TV. Art clanged pots in the other room, preparing Christmas Eve dinner while Gretchen alternated bringing everyone hot cocoa and aiding him in the kitchen.

This should be bliss—a holiday to remember. But instead, Charlie's heart weighed a thousand pounds, and all she could think about were the question marks shadowing the evening. So many unknowns right around the corner...about the shelter. About Blake. About Tori. What was going to happen? The word *trust* kept ricocheting around her heart, but it just bounced off all the wary guards she had in place, unable to land and plant roots.

Charlie stared into the tree as the twinkle lights blurred. There were plenty of reasons to hope—Mark still hadn't gotten back to Blake, so the sale might not go through. Or the fund-raisers might have been successful enough to cover relocating the shelter if it did. Rachel was supposed to update her on the books anytime now.

"Look what I found." Gretchen blitzed into the room, holding a small cardboard box. Blake's name was written in Sharpie across the top.

Charlie's eyes widened, and she stiffened on the couch. Was that the ornament? The one he'd chosen eight years ago and never hung?

"I thought it might be time to bring this out." Gretchen handed the box to Charlie, then settled on the couch beside her. The comforting aromas of cinnamon and vanilla wafted over Charlie, tugging her back to her teen years.

To the years with Blake.

"I think it might mean something to you now." Gretchen tapped the box. "Go on. Open it."

Charlie lifted the flaps and carefully removed a square ornament. "A yearbook." She turned it over, running her finger over the spine of the faux book. Her voice deepened with suppressed emotion. "With our graduating class year on the side."

"And something else written on the back." Gretchen pointed to small letters, slightly smudged.

Charlie held it closer to read.

Most Likely to End Up Together.

Her eyes stung with instant tears. Unlike the same message written in the snow the other day, this one held an entirely different truth. This wasn't an attempt to manipulate or matchmake. This was genuine. Blake had been a twenty-two-year-old college student when he chose the ornament and wrote on the back. Had this been a small way for him to express how he felt about her? It seemed so much more heartfelt and intentional than the reckless, impulsive invitation to run away with him.

Why hadn't he ever said anything?

"I never brought this out before, because you didn't seem in a good place to see it. But when I got your old yearbook out the other day and remembered that title… well." Gretchen patted Charlie's knee. "It meant something to Blake, too, honey. Maybe—just maybe—you misunderstood him all this time."

Charlie held the ornament by its thick gold thread and watched it spin. Maybe she had. But it was too late. Wasn't that their more accurate title—Most Likely to Be Too Late? Blake was leaving and would once again be dragging a trail of heartache in his wake. Heartache over his absence and now Tori's, too—not to mention the heartache of Paradise Paws most likely closing.

She took a deep breath, then set the ornament back into the box and closed the lid. She handed it to Gretchen. "I've got to go take Tori to meet Blake."

Gretchen's lips pursed slightly, but she just accepted the box back, then moved her legs out of the way for Charlie to scoot past.

The doorbell rang before she could coax Tori from her game of UNO. Detouring to the foyer, Charlie tugged open the front door.

Rachel stood on the front stoop, holding a small potted poinsettia.

"Oh, hey, come on in." Charlie stepped aside. "I didn't know you were coming."

"Merry Christmas." Rachel paused to brush the snow off her scarf, then stepped inside, shivering. "I brought this for Gretchen."

"She'll love it." Charlie took the plant from her friend and shut the door. "Everyone is in the living room. Come get warm by the fire. I've got to meet someone in a few minutes, but you're welcome to stay." She couldn't bear to even say Blake's name in front of Rachel right now— not with Paradise Paws's fate so up in the air.

"I can't stay too long, either." Rachel avoided Charlie's eyes as she stomped her feet on the entry mat. "Be careful out there—it's getting colder."

"Maybe it'll be a white Christmas." Charlie shifted the poinsettia in her arms and smiled…then realized her friend wasn't smiling back. "But that's not why you're here."

"I hate to be the bearer of bad news." Rachel lowered her voice, craning to see over Charlie's shoulder as the teens' laughter echoed from the living room. "But I just ran the numbers. Both fund-raisers did better than I expected, but we earned about enough to pay the bills for a few months. Or possibly pay rent in a new, more expensive location, for one month. Definitely not both."

Charlie's last hopes sank. Christmas seemed to be getting bleaker, and not because of the brutal weather. It was official. If Blake made the sale, that would be it for the shelter. Come January, they'd be scrambling to find owners for the existing dogs—or worse.

Charlie stared into the arrangement of bright red leaves in her arms. It was time to tell the girls about Paradise Paws.

Chapter Eighteen

❦

"But why can't the new owner just give Rachel the same cheaper rent price that Mr. Raines gives the shelter?" Tori twisted in the front seat of Charlie's SUV to face her. "Wouldn't that fix everything?"

"Because the new owner is starting a different kind of business after he buys the land. Coffee shops and dogs don't really mix." Charlie kept her eyes on the road, giving her a welcome reprieve from the direct emotion of the last twenty minutes of conversation.

She'd briefly sat all four girls down with Gretchen and Rachel and explained that the shelter was likely going to close next month. That the fund-raisers hadn't gone far enough to cover what they'd hoped, and it wasn't looking good if Mr. Raines ended up selling. Gretchen, as usual, calmly capped off the conversation with encouragement for the teens to pray for provision.

Charlie turned on her blinker as she navigated toward the Sweet Briar Café. She hadn't had the heart to tell any of them that she'd been praying for weeks, to no avail. She didn't want to douse the girls' developing faith because of her own trust issues. Of course, she'd left out the detail about Blake's direct involvement. That would be the worst timing possible, with his big reveal planned.

At Gretchen's subtle urging, the other teens had stayed home to finish helping Art with dinner, though Nadia kept shooting them suspicious glances as Charlie and Tori headed out with the promise of bringing back holiday milkshakes for everyone. She knew Blake wouldn't want the whole crowd at the café during his announcement, but hopefully it'd be something to celebrate together afterward.

Tori faced forward again as flakes of snow pelted the windshield. "The big company can't just pick another property?"

She wished Blake would—or rather, Blake's boss. But from the business side of things, she saw the appeal. "I think the new company really wants this property because of the scenery. The pond and the hills…it's the perfect spot for a coffee shop and event venue."

"But Mr. Raines hasn't agreed to sell yet?"

"Not yet. But I think it's just a matter of time. That's why Ms. Rachel came over and we told you guys tonight—once we realized the fund-raisers hadn't raised enough money to help the shelter, we didn't want you caught off guard after the holidays."

Tori worked her bottom lip. "What's going to happen to Waffles?"

"I don't know." Charlie held back her sigh of discouragement. She hated that she couldn't give better answers. But she *could* offer hope—the same hope she was trying to hold on to herself. "Maybe someone in the area will adopt him and let you visit." Or maybe Tori would end up moving away with Blake and it wouldn't matter.

Both thoughts felt equally depressing.

"Maybe." Tori's voice held as much doubt as Charlie's heart. "I don't see why things have to change."

"Me neither, honey. Change isn't always fun." And there was a lot more coming the young girl's way. Would she think it positive or negative? Regardless, right now they needed to shift focus to Blake's upcoming announcement and trust that the rest would work out. Charlie tightened her grip on the steering wheel. There was that word again—*trust*. She couldn't get away from it.

She parked in front of the café and turned to face the younger girl. "We're not going to let this ruin our Christmas, okay?"

Tori nodded slowly as she unbuckled her seat belt. "I'll try."

She opened her car door and glanced inside the diner, spying Blake's dark hair through the glass at a window table. "Let's go get that milkshake. I think someone inside has some good news for you."

Blake hadn't had an exact image in his mind of how this big reveal was going to go, but it hadn't included a downcast Tori sitting in a nearly empty diner, fiddling with her straw wrapper as "White Christmas" drifted over the café speakers. It was Christmas Eve—why wasn't she more excited? Or looking at him, for that matter? In fact, she seemed like she'd rather be anywhere else.

He cleared his throat, drumming his fingers on the table. "Is your milkshake good?"

She nodded, folding the wrapper into thirds.

He glanced at Charlie, whose brown eyes widened slightly as she nodded her encouragement for him to dive in. His stomach fluttered. Not with butterflies—this felt more like a flying murder of crows. He took a deep breath, then tried to still his frenetic tapping. "Tori, I have some news for you."

"Is it about the milkshake? Everyone seems to be making them a pretty big deal." She stirred the thick shake with her straw and shrugged.

"No." He snorted back a laugh. "It's a lot better news than that."

Beside Tori, Charlie stilled, as if bracing for the big moment. His heart thudded, and a collage of future hopes flooded his mind. Holiday meals with Tori and him together as a family. Buying school supplies. Movie nights on weekends with popcorn. Him giving fatherly advice about relationships. Sitting in church together on Sundays. Their worlds were both about to drastically change.

That was, if he could get the words out.

He swallowed and took the leap. "I'm your uncle."

"What?" Her hands stilled on the straw wrapper.

"I'm your uncle. I've been in town these last few weeks to get to know you."

"You're my uncle." She repeated his words, her voice dry and monotone and not at all like he'd hoped.

He shot a helpless look at Charlie, who turned to Tori. "Hey," she said, smoothing Tori's long hair behind her shoulder, her tone gentle and patient. "Isn't that good news? You have family!"

"I don't understand. Why didn't you tell me sooner?" *Now* she looked at him, but not with the joy he'd prayed for. Sparks of something he couldn't quite place lit her eyes.

"I've only known for about a month, myself. So I was waiting for the right time." He pulled his hands into his lap and cracked his knuckles. "I wanted you to get to know me first. And then, well…we didn't have the best start."

Thankfully she nodded, as if that part at least made sense. "Only for a month? That's…like, something out of a movie, isn't it?"

"Feels that way, doesn't it?" Charlie laid a sympathetic hand on Tori's shoulder. "We realize you'll have a lot of questions, and that's okay."

"So you know my mom? Or my dad?" Tori blinked. "Wait, you're my uncle. So you're my mom's…brother. Or my dad's brother."

"Right. Your mother's brother." So much to process on so many levels. He had to be patient. He'd had weeks to let the news soak in—she'd had minutes. He released his nervous breath. "I'd really like to become your guardian, Tori. Be a family."

There. It was all out. Weeks of secrets, spread across the sticky diner table between them. Whatever happened from here was outside his control. But it didn't stop him from hoping for the best.

Tori chewed on her bottom lip, avoiding his gaze as she stirred the pink concoction in her tall glass. "Do I have to decide right now?"

"Of course not." Blake hesitated. Apparently, she didn't find the news to be the best Christmas gift ever, like he'd hoped. Was she still wary of him? Their dynamic had been so much better lately.

Their waitress came and topped off his coffee, giving him time to shoot Charlie a "help me" look.

Lowering her voice, Charlie gently asked, "What are you thinking, Tor?"

"That Mr.…that Blake… I mean, Uncle… *You* don't

live here." She pushed aside her milkshake, her voice pitching. "And I don't want to move."

He nodded slowly. "That's true. We would have to go to Colorado when this was all said and done. My job needs me." More like he needed the job, but with a little time, maybe he could find a way to get them back to Tulip Mound. He just couldn't offer that hope before he knew for sure.

He rushed on before Tori could stress further. "But it would take a while—the adoption process is lengthy. We're not talking about leaving next week or anything sudden. I have to go back sooner, but you wouldn't. Not yet."

The teen remained silent, her lips pursing together as if holding back a volcano.

Is she okay? He mouthed the words at Charlie as Tori continued to stare at the tabletop, her face blank and neutral despite the firm press on her mouth.

"I was trying to avoid this, but we might as well talk about all of it." Charlie braced her forearms on the table. "Blake, Tori knows about the shelter."

Blake's heart dropped. "You told her?"

Charlie nodded. "Tonight. Rachel came over with the news that the fund-raisers hadn't done well enough, so Gretchen and I talked to the girls." She nudged Tori. "That's why you're upset, isn't it?"

At her nod of confirmation, Blake's throat knotted. No wonder the younger girl had such a guardedness in her eyes ever since walking in the diner. He was the bad guy again. She'd already written him off—just like Charlie.

Indignation churned. How could Charlie tell Tori something that big without giving him a heads-up, especially after agreeing to help him?

Then the frustration was immediately replaced with the reminder that he was responsible. He'd put it off for too long. Hadn't Charlie and Anita both encouraged him to talk to Tori ASAP? If he'd been honest up front, they could have worked through it sooner.

He took a steadying breath. "Look, Tori, I don't blame you for being upset with me about the shelter."

Charlie reached across the table, her eyes widening. "Blake, wait—"

"No, I think you've said plenty already." He barreled forward. "Yes, I'm here to purchase the land from Mr. Raines. And it looks like doing so might shut down the shelter if they can't relocate."

"*You're* the one buying the shelter?" Tori frowned, confusion highlighting her expression. "I don't understand. You're the coffee shop?"

He nodded, even as a nauseous feeling seeped into his stomach. "I work for the business that wants to purchase the shelter's land, yes."

"So the shelter is closing…and it's *your* fault." Her voice shook with betrayal. "My *uncle's* fault."

Wait. What was happening? "I thought you knew that." Confusion churned, and he looked desperately at Charlie. "You just said she knew about the shelter!"

"She knows the shelter is in financial trouble and didn't get the funds it needed to survive relocating." Charlie pressed her fingers against the bridge of her nose, eyes closed. "*Not* the part about your involvement."

Oh, no. Blake opened his mouth, but it was too late.

"What?" Tori erupted from the booth, knocking over her milkshake. Pink ice cream puddled across the wooden surface. She stood with both hands planted on her hips and she glared—this time at Charlie. "You knew, *too*?" Her brows furrowed together as tears lit her eyes.

Charlie's expression broke. "Tori, it's complicated—"

"Apparently everything with adults is just so *complicated*." Her tone mocked. "I hope I never grow up." She pushed away from the table and ran out the door of the café.

Blake immediately stood to go after her, but Charlie grasped his forearm, tugging him back. "No. Give her a minute. She just needs a breath."

He'd really messed up. He looked out the window at Tori standing beneath the lamplight, arms hugging herself. "But it's cold outside." It'd stopped snowing, but the wind chill was freezing.

"Trust me, pushing her to talk right now—with either of us—will only do more harm than good." Charlie began piling napkins on top of the milkshake mess. "She needs to cool off. That was a lot of information at once."

"You mean a lot of bad news at once." Blake watched the melting ice cream run toward his coffee cup. "I can't believe I told on myself…and I can't believe I assumed you told on *me*." He swallowed. "I'm really sorry."

"It is what it is. At least it's all out now." Charlie craned her neck to check on Tori, still under the streetlight. He followed her gaze, but Tori's bent head kept her hair like a curtain hiding her face—and her feelings. "Just give her some time."

He helped Charlie wad up the soaked napkins, trying to read her stoic face as she sopped up more ice cream. Then he stood and grabbed an abandoned tray from a nearby table and piled the napkins on top. "I'll pay and get the rest of this. Why don't you go ahead and take her back to Tulip House, where it's warm?"

Charlie surrendered the rest of the napkins and headed out without a word. Blake dropped a bill on the table, then turned to the nearby trash can with the full tray, his steps heavy. He didn't know what he'd do the rest of the night. He'd envisioned bringing gifts over to Tulip House for all the girls, celebrating the good news of his new family with sparkling cider. But now… Was he just destined to be alone?

He tossed the napkins inside the full bin and stood mutely by the trash can as the scents of leftover onions and grease filled his senses. He'd successfully made this a Christmas to remember—just not in the way he'd wanted.

"Blake!"

He turned as Charlie rushed back in, her eyes wide and hair windblown. She crashed into him before he could catch her, face panicked. She gripped both his arms. "Tori's gone."

Chapter Nineteen

Charlie burst through the front door of Tulip House, her heart threatening to leap out of her throat. How could they have lost Tori? With Blake on her heels, they strode into the kitchen, where Art was dishing up Christmas dinner and the teens were setting the big table.

"Have you guys seen Tori?" But even as Charlie's eyes bounced from one dark-haired head to the other two blond ones, she knew Tori wasn't with the girls.

Gretchen looked down from her perch on a stepladder, where she was pulling out the holiday linens from a high cabinet over the dishwasher. "Isn't she with you?"

Charlie's heart stuttered. "Not anymore." She'd been so sure Tori had simply headed the few blocks home on her own, and they'd just missed her on the drive back. Now she was out there, somewhere in the cold, angry and alone.

Her legs felt wobbly. Some CASA volunteer she was. Her charge was out in the freezing wind chill with nothing more than a scarf and puffy jacket.

Blake laid a steadying hand on her shoulder. "Don't panic."

"Who's panicking?" Gretchen scurried down the ladder, arms full of folded red and green fabric. "What's going on?"

Art turned from the island, a ladle dripping with gravy hovering over the pan of chicken and dressing. "Tori's missing?"

Forks clattered on the table as the teens registered the news. *"What?"* The three spoke at once.

"She got upset and walked out of the diner after Blake told her he was her uncle. I thought she was just going to get some fresh air, but she'd vanished by the time we paid and came out." The words tumbled from Charlie's lips before she could remember the teenagers didn't have the full context like Gretchen and Art.

Riley gasped.

"Say *what*?" Nadia's eyebrows shot up.

"You're her *uncle*?" Sabrina's mouth gaped open.

Blake nodded, shifting uncomfortably beside Charlie. "You're all taking it a bit better than she did."

"We can come back to the rest later." Charlie gripped Blake's arm in warning. This wasn't the time to tell the other parts of the story. Hopefully he wasn't going to—

"That's not all." He shuffled his feet across the worn kitchen floor, and Charlie groaned. He shot her a pointed stare. "I have to get this out—look what happened last time when I avoided it."

She couldn't argue there.

He took a deep breath and faced the girls. "I'm the one responsible for Paradise Paws being sold."

Three sets of teen eyes narrowed at once. "Say *what*?" Nadia asked again. She crossed her arms over her chest.

Blake continued. "I work for the buyer looking to purchase the property. When Tori realized that, she got really upset."

"I can see why," Sabrina muttered under her breath. "Being related to a traitor and all."

So they were back to the Benedict Arnold speech. "Sabrina, that's enough." Charlie pointed at the girls, hyperaware of the minutes ticking past on the clock. "Can we all please forget about that right now and focus on the fact that Tori is missing?"

Something fierce and protective crossed Nadia's face, and she strode purposefully toward the coatrack. "I'm going after her."

A flurry of green plaid napkins piled onto the table as Sabrina eagerly abandoned her chore and pushed past Blake. "I'm coming, too!"

Riley started after them, knocking into a kitchen chair. "Wait for—"

Art dropped his ladle. "Girls, you can't just—"

Gretchen's two-fingered whistle split the air, effectively halting the jumble of voices and panic meshing together across the kitchen. "*Everyone*, wait. You will do as you're told."

Even Charlie's hand stilled on its reach for the doorknob. Gretchen rarely used her mama voice, but when she did, Charlie was pretty sure even the neighborhood cats sat up straight.

"Art and I will go look for Tori." Gretchen pointed at Nadia. "You will stir the gravy."

Nadia's chin lifted, but she didn't argue.

"You both will finish setting the table…" She pointed at the twins. "And you two—" her finger flicked between Blake and Charlie "—come with me outside. Tell me exactly what happened."

* * *

"You know, I've always supported Gretchen's decision not to give the girls cell phone privileges, but I sure wish Tori had one right about now." Charlie wiped at her red-rimmed eyes as she perched on the couch—noticeably a full cushion away from Blake. "I hate to say this, but I almost wouldn't be as worried if it was Nadia, or even Sabrina or Riley, out there."

"How do you mean?" Blake asked. After getting the whole story, Gretchen and Art had instructed them to stay home with the teens to make sure they didn't leave, too, and promised they'd be back with Tori as soon as possible. It'd already been over half an hour—he couldn't stop looking at his watch.

"They're older and more savvy." Charlie glanced over her shoulder toward the cracked door leading to the hallway, where dishes clattered as the teens worked in the kitchen. "Tori is still naive in so many ways. She hasn't let life harden her yet, you know?"

"She might now, thanks to me." Blake dragged his hand over his jaw. "I couldn't have handled that conversation any worse." He couldn't keep from replaying the whole night in his head.

How had things gotten so messed up so quickly?

Charlie's eyes shone like glass. "It's my fault. I should have let you go after her when you started to."

"That'd all be irrelevant if I had told her the truth a long time ago, like you and Anita suggested." Blake shook his head. "I kept telling myself it was for Tori's own good to drag out who I was, but I was just being selfish."

"Maybe it was both." Charlie pulled her knees up to her chest.

Blake squinted at her, unsure if that was a jab or an olive branch.

"You believed it was best for her—*and* you were scared. Which made you act accordingly."

"You've got me all figured out, huh?"

"I've always known you, Blake." Her quiet words somehow both tempered and ignited something in his spirit.

He swallowed against the rise of emotion. "I didn't handle this thing with me and you well, either. When I got back to Tulip Mound, everything hit at once. All the things I'd tried to stuff down for years blasted straight to the surface, and I couldn't hide anymore."

Like how much he'd missed her. How much he wanted to be her friend again. To be more than a friend, really— if he wasn't already permanently branded the bad guy.

Regret pinched. He'd tried so hard to force a family— first with Charlie, years ago, then with Tori, all while not giving any credence to their own dreams, plans or goals. He'd just barreled in, dropped what he wanted in everyone's lap and expected them to immediately comply.

Would he ever learn?

"I'm sorry. For the way I've handled all of this. And for my role with Jitter Mugs… I wish there was a different way." He shrugged. "But right now, all I want is to know Tori is safe."

Charlie clutched a throw pillow against her knees. "What if she doesn't come back, Blake?"

He had the same fear, which the Lord had heard multiple times from him in the past hour. "We have to trust that she will."

Charlie rolled in her lower lip. "Always with that word."

The front door banged open, and Gretchen and Art

rushed straight into the living room. "She wasn't at the park or the animal shelter. Or at her favorite restaurant." Gretchen tugged at her thick scarf, her cheeks flushed with cold. "We're not sure where else to check."

"The shelter!" Blake jumped to his feet, the couch sliding a foot behind him at his abrupt escape. "That's it. Let's go." Of course. It seemed obvious now. His heart thundered.

"Son, we just said she wasn't there." Art rested one hand on Blake's shoulder, concern etching his expression. "I think it's time we alert the police."

"No, I heard you. I just have an idea." His eyes searched Charlie's, and he hoped—prayed—he was right. "Call Rachel. Have her meet us at Paradise Paws." He took a deep breath. "I know how to find her."

A few minutes later, Rachel's dark brow furrowed as they all crowded on the front porch under the dim overhead light as she unlocked the door. "Is there anything else I can do to help? I can't believe this happened."

"It's going to be okay. We'll find her." Blake was back to his business tone, the incredibly confident, take-charge one that originally had annoyed Charlie when he first arrived back in Tulip Mound but now gave her hope that maybe he was right.

Together, they followed Rachel inside. Charlie flipped on the light switch, illuminating the dim hallway leading to Rachel's office and a dusty fern that wasn't surviving the winter well. Then she shivered inside her jacket as the cold air followed them in.

"We already looked here," Gretchen reminded them, hovering in the doorway of the lobby. Art had stayed back with the girls at Tulip House, hoping to salvage dinner and have a hot meal ready for Tori once they found her. "We walked around the front of the property and called for her, but only the dogs barked at us. She's not here."

"Speaking of the dogs—where's Waffles?" Blake sneezed, then grabbed a tissue from the box on the foyer end table. With watery eyes, he looked expectantly at Rachel.

She pointed to another door at the far end of the foyer building. "That leads to the indoor kennel. It's too cold to keep them outside on nights like this."

He started in the direction she'd pointed, but Charlie couldn't wonder any longer. She tugged at his arm, pulling him slightly aside as Gretchen shut the front door to block the wind. "Blake, wait. What are you doing?"

He looked down at her, his eyes full of fear and hope and a dozen other things she didn't have time to fully evaluate. He touched her chin briefly, then seemed to catch himself and lowered his hand to his side. "Waffles loves hide-and-seek, remember?"

Chapter Twenty

Charlie watched as Blake clipped the end of a leash onto Waffles's collar, paused to sneeze twice into his arm, then stood, the part-hound looking as tired and droopy as his ears. "Okay, boy," Blake said. "Hide-and-seek time. Find Tori."

Rachel pressed closer to Charlie as they all filed through the building back toward the foyer. "He does know that's not Lassie, right? And there's not a well on this property?"

Charlie snorted, hanging back a step to observe. "They do play hide-and-seek a lot." It'd been a long shot the moment Blake suggested it, but her hopes had gotten up. Now Waffles just looked annoyed at having been roused from his warm bed.

"But he doesn't know commands like that. He doesn't realize he's in a game." Rachel pursed her lips as Blake tugged on the leash. Waffles only sat in response, looking up at Blake with disdain as he sneezed a third time. Rachel shook her head. "Waffles needs a scent to follow. Do you have anything of Tori's?"

"No, she—" Then Charlie remembered glimpsing

something purple in her car earlier that evening. "Wait. I think she left a hoodie in my back seat!"

"That'd be perfect." Rachel clapped her hands together.

"I'll get it!" Gretchen scurried outside, the door banging behind her.

Despite his allergy-watery eyes, Blake bent over, scratching Waffles's head as they waited. "This is your moment, man. We need you."

Gretchen returned, Tori's purple hoodie in hand. She gave it to Blake, who held it out to Waffles.

"Where is she?" He pulled it away, then offered the hoodie a second time. "You always find her. Legend has it, she never wins this game."

Waffles sniffed the jacket without much interest, then hesitated and sniffed again. His body tensed, and his tail wagged.

"That's it." Blake carried the hoodie toward the back door. "Where is she?"

A lump knotted in Charlie's throat. Was this really going to work? Where would they even start? She breathed a prayer, still afraid to fully hope. To trust.

Then Waffles tugged on the leash and whined. Blake's eyes widened. "Let's go!"

"We'll stay up here so we don't distract Waffles." Rachel gestured between herself and Gretchen. "And we'll keep an eye out front in case Tori happens to come that way."

They split up, Blake and Charlie following a suddenly eager Waffles out the back door, while Rachel and Gretchen retreated to the front porch.

Waffles pulled Blake down the stairs, nose pressing against the steps, then came to an abrupt halt as his nose touched snow.

"I wondered if that would throw him off." Blake

sighed. "Come on, boy, don't give up." He offered the hoodie again, and Waffles began leading them in a zig-zag pattern around the powdery yard.

They walked for several minutes in silence, following Waffles as he paused occasionally to sniff the hoodie and then lift his nose to the frigid night air.

"You know, Tori's reaction to all this wasn't exactly what I'd hoped." Blake continued following Waffles's lead, offering more leash. "But it taught me something kinda priceless."

Charlie looked up at his strong profile, at the stubble covering his jaw, and felt a rush of familiarity. The new Blake that had come back to Tulip Mound seemed to have finally meshed into this man standing before her. One she sort of wanted to throttle for all the trouble he had caused, but who also made her want to wrap him into a big hug, because he was still Blake underneath that pro-verbial starched-suit exterior. He was still her friend.

And right now, he looked like he needed a friend.

If that was all they could ever be, she could do that much. At least for tonight.

She took a deep breath, then wrapped her arm through his. He startled, looking down at her in surprise. She held his arm tighter. "It's cold." That was the only rea-son she could give, and it was at least a partially honest one. Which only made her worry more about Tori being out in the elements. "Back to your story." This wasn't the time to process her own feelings. They needed to focus on Tori. "What'd you realize?"

"It taught me that Tori can't fill this need I have for acceptance, any more than I can fill it for her." Blake shrugged. "I'd love to be a father to her, but more than that, I want to make sure she knows that God is her Heavenly Father—and mine." His Adam's apple bobbed above his buttoned jacket. "He always was, even when earthly dads don't do too good of a job."

Emmanuel. God with us.

Emotion welled in Charlie's chest. "Blake…" A dozen thoughts roiled in her mind, like the time Gretchen had reminded her Blake wasn't a bad guy. Maybe he wasn't. Maybe he was still just her old friend who had gotten into a difficult position—a rock-and-hard-place-type scenario.

Realizing that didn't remove the obstacles between them. But for the first time, it gave her a little sympathy for his situation, rather than only seeing her own.

Waffles suddenly tugged them in a different direction, closer toward the pond. Blake adjusted his grip on the leash. "I hope I get a chance to remind Tori of that."

"You will." She offered a fledgling smile. "See? It's my turn to trust."

"How's that going for you?" He glanced down, his expression amused. "Because you look a little pale."

"Trusting is hard work." She tried to laugh, but it came out sounding more like a half snort, half cry. "I've had a similar realization of my own. I'm always afraid people are going to leave…and now Tori's missing, and you're going back to Colorado." She inhaled deeply and released it, her breath a white puff of air in the night chill. "But I'm okay. Because, like you just said—our Heavenly Father never leaves me."

Blake stilled, his arm tensing beneath her grip. "I really am sorry about the shelter. I never came here with the intention for that to happen. You know that, right?"

"I do." Charlie believed him—now. Blake wasn't cruel. He was just trying to do the right thing for his niece—and that had to come first. It was honorable, if not incredibly unfortunate. "I just wish the fund-raisers had been more successful. So many people came out to support Paradise Paws, and several dogs even got adopted. But the cash flow just wasn't there."

Blake stopped short, and a sudden look breached the shadows on his face—one Charlie couldn't quite decipher. She tugged at his elbow. "What? You look like you have an idea."

He resumed walking slowly. "I think I do. You know, maybe the fund-raisers—"

Waffles suddenly lunged forward, pulling Blake with him. The anxious dog barreled straight toward the storage building halfway across the yard, letting out a yippy howl along the way.

Charlie sucked in a burst of cold air as Waffles pawed at the shut door. She hurried to catch up, heart thundering. "Do you think…?"

Blake tugged at the door, but it didn't budge. "Is it locked?"

She shook her head. "Rachel keeps it unlocked, because it's such a hassle to remember the key when she's trying to refill the food bins."

Blake handed her Waffles's leash, gripped the knob with two hands and wrenched backward. The door flung open with a reluctant groan, the entire building trembling at the force.

Waffles barked and flung himself inside the dark space first, his tongue eagerly licking a pale face framed with two wide blue eyes.

Tori.

They'd found her. She was safe.

Blake automatically pulled Tori into a hug before he realized she might not want one from him. He quickly stepped back, but Tori lunged forward, closing the distance between them, and gripped his waist with her skinny arms. "You found me."

He hugged her in return, relief coursing through his veins so hard he shook. The back of her jacket was freezing cold. Would she have made it through the night? He shook away the thought. "Waffles found you, technically."

Tori eased away, wiping tears from her flushed cheeks with the back of her glove. "How did you know?"

He grinned, feeling it wobble from leftover adrenaline. "I remembered your games. You never win, right?"

Waffles barked, and Tori laughed through her leftover tears. Charlie pulled her into a hug next. "I'm so glad you're okay. What happened? We've been looking for you for hours."

"I'm sorry I ran away." Tori bit down on her lower lip. "I didn't mean to make everyone worry. I wanted to see Waffles, because after you told me about the shelter being sold, I was scared it would be too late. I didn't even think about it being locked up tonight."

Regret knocked, along with more than a little guilt. He should have handled things so differently. Then he noticed she was standing on one foot. "Wait a second. Are you hurt?"

"I twisted my ankle on the front porch steps after I realized no one was here." Tori wobbled, her left ankle raised. "I couldn't walk back to the Sweet Briar Café, and I was so cold at that point, I thought I'd try to warm up while I figured out what to do next. I know this storage shed is usually unlocked. But the wind slammed the door shut behind me, and I couldn't get back out."

"You must have been so scared." Charlie ran her hand over Tori's hair, worry pinching her brow.

"It definitely wasn't fun in there." Tori sniffed, her eyes bloodshot. "But it's my fault. I shouldn't have left like that."

Blake steadied her with a hand on her shoulder as the younger girl continued to stand like a winter flamingo. There was so much they all needed to talk about, so much to process. The last thing Blake wanted was for her to blame all this on herself. But as she'd realized—and as he finally had as well, eight years later—running away from hard things never solved them. It just made them worse.

As if reading his mind, Charlie picked up Waffles's leash. "I think we've all learned some lessons tonight. Let's get you home so we can warm up and eat. I believe there's some presents waiting on you, too." She hesitated, her gaze flittering from Tori to her sore ankle. "Maybe I can give you a piggyback ride."

"I've got her." Blake scooped Tori up carefully into his arms. And as she wrapped her arms around his neck and buried her face in his shoulder, every doubt Blake had ever had about being a father immediately melted away as a voracious urge to protect her surged within him.

But that included following one more instinct.

He carried Tori to the back porch of the shelter, then set her down in front of the door, hanging back two stairs down so they were eye level. He waited a beat, part of him not wanting to make the suggestion but knowing deep down it made the most sense.

"I was thinking." He took a deep breath. No more projecting his own past and needs onto Tori. It was time to let go and see what God had for them. "Instead of you deciding right now about me officially adopting you... what if I could just be your uncle for a while?"

Surprise, followed by a wave of relief, crashed over her

face. She swiped her hair out of her eyes with a gloved hand. "Are you sure?"

"I'm sure I want what's best for you. And right now, I think taking you away from this sweet setup you've got at Tulip House isn't ideal." He shrugged, though the notion broke his heart a little. But this wasn't about him— it was about her. Wasn't that the first step to parenting? "There's no reason we can't ease into this."

Charlie moved to Tori's side, wrapping one arm around her shoulders as Waffles settled on the snowy deck at Tori's feet. "As your CASA volunteer, I think that's a great idea." Her approving nod confirmed all Blake needed to know.

Tori reached down to pet Waffles's floppy ears, her voice small. "But will you be long-distance?"

"For a while. But I can visit." He climbed the top two steps slowly, meeting Charlie's gaze over Tori's head, and dared to offer a smile. "And who knows what the future holds?" He needed time to flesh out his idea, the one he hadn't had a chance to tell Charlie about. But maybe that was for the best. Maybe he needed to make it official before he got anyone's hopes up. Maybe that was why—in the Lord's providence—Mark hadn't gotten back to him yet. It gave him time to put some numbers together—

Then his cell rang from his pocket.

Blake quickly pulled it free, muffling a sneeze into his elbow before saying hello.

"Mr. Bryant? Mark Raines." The younger guy's voice was rushed. "I'm sorry to bother you on Christmas Eve, but I hated to leave you hanging any longer."

Here it was. His answer—finally. And with the worst timing possible.

Blake glanced over at Charlie as she enveloped Tori

into a hug so big, the girl practically disappeared. "Actually, it's not a good time right—"

"I just wanted to let you know I officially accept the offer."

Christmas afternoon, Charlie's slice of apple pie sat untouched on the coffee table before her, partly because she was still full of Art's delicious Christmas lunch they'd feasted on an hour ago, partly because she knew Mark Raines had accepted Blake's offer last night...and partly because Blake's plane would be leaving in less than twenty-four hours. It felt so unfair that they'd finally found their way into a fledgling friendship and, once again—it was too late. Of course he'd be back to visit Tori often, but it wouldn't be the same. His home was in Colorado.

And one day, eventually, Tori's would be, too.

As much as she wanted to hold on to the joy of finding Tori safe and sound last night—their own Christmas miracle—Charlie couldn't help but wish for one more.

Blake was late for Christmas presents, though he'd shot her a quick text earlier that morning about trying to secure a last-minute gift and not to wait on him. Surely he'd show up—he wouldn't do that to Tori. But what could be keeping him so long?

Across the living room, the girls took turns checking the name tags on the pile of gifts under the tree while Gretchen paced, occasionally shaking various snow globes in her collection and watching the flakes fall as if she, too, were trying to distract herself. Were they all concerned about Blake's absence? Charlie checked the time again on her phone just as the front door burst open.

She sat upright on the couch as Art and Blake strode purposefully inside the room. Blake's cheeks were flushed red from the cold, and his eyes shone over the top of his blue fisherman's sweater. "Sorry I'm late, you guys." He rushed straight to the television set across the room and lowered his computer bag to the rug. "Art, give me a hand here, will you?"

Without waiting for a reply, he began opening his laptop and connecting cables while Art ran a long one to the back of the TV monitor. Then Blake knelt by the coffee table with his laptop, scooting Charlie's pie plate out of the way. "I have a gift."

"For who?" Nadia asked suspiciously as the four girls crept closer to the TV.

"I guess that depends." Blake shot Charlie a look she couldn't quite read, then began typing. A PowerPoint presentation filled his screen, then appeared on the television. Various color-coded charts and graphs stood out against a white background.

Tori frowned. "I don't get it."

"Yeah, this is cool and all, but I'll give you a hint. Teenagers prefer new clothes or makeup." Nadia arched her brow at him as she moved from the floor to the couch by Charlie.

"Girls." Gretchen shushed them. "Give him a chance."

Art chuckled.

Blake continued, unaffected. "These are the numbers I put together from the fund-raisers. You'll see I have crowd participation here…" He jumped up and pointed to one of the colored squares on the TV screen. "Donations received here, and goods purchased here."

The fund-raisers? But why? Charlie felt as confused as Tori looked. She squinted as Blake pointed to the next slide, which had broken the two fund-raisers into separate charts with similar information. They already knew the fund-raisers had been a flop. Why was he making that fact color-coded and official?

As if reading her thoughts, Blake went on. "As we all learned yesterday, the fund-raisers weren't successful in reaching their goals. And Mr. Raines officially accepted the offer from Jitter Mugs."

Okay, now she was really struggling to remember Blake wasn't the bad guy.

"So that's it, then? No more shelter?" Nadia's tone hardened. She shot Charlie a glance. "You really should teach this man how to Christmas shop."

"Hang on." Blake laughed, a secret shining in his eyes like a teasing spotlight. "There's one more slide left, you guys." He tapped a key on his laptop, and a new image filled the screen. "Don't judge my artwork, either."

An amateur mock-up of a building nestled among sprawling green hills and a blue pond lit the TV. Cartoon dogs ran around the grounds while stick-figure customers stood about, holding what resembled tiny spaceships. Charlie tilted her head to one side. Or maybe those were coffee cups.

"Is that Waffles?" Tori inched closer to the TV. "I recognize those long ears."

"That is Waffles," Blake confirmed. "And this is the same presentation I just gave to my boss via Zoom back at the Hummingbird Inn. He was so happy to hear the deal on the land finally went through, he didn't mind talking to me on Christmas."

"What's going on, Blake?" Hope sprang in Charlie's chest, so fragile she dared not breathe. The room silenced. Even Art leaned in closer, his calm, stoic presence radiating energy.

"The numbers don't lie." Blake pointed to the screen.

"I was able to convince him that a new franchise, combining the traditional shop with the shelter, would go a long way with the residents of Tulip Mound. They love coffee, but they really love dogs." He shrugged a little. "Of course, I also might have exaggerated a little about a potential boycott if they shut down Paradise Paws."

He'd done it. He'd saved the shelter. The fragile sprig of hope blossomed into a full burst of joy. Without thinking, Charlie stood and launched herself at Blake in a hug. His arms immediately encircled her, and she inhaled the scents of evergreen and spice and everything uniquely him. "Thank you," she breathed as excited chatter filled the room.

As she pulled away, the heavy weight of his arm around her waist reminded her of one hard remaining truth—they would get to keep the shelter. But they were still losing Blake. *She* was still losing Blake. Her joy dimmed.

"There's one more detail you might be interested in." Blake clicked to the next slide, which featured a big red question mark. "Being such a unique concept, Jitter Mugs will need an invested manager for this particular franchise. One who knows the business—and the area—really well."

The room fell so quiet, Charlie could almost hear the snowflakes falling in Gretchen's snow globes.

"*Me*, you guys." Blake huffed in mock exasperation. "It's me. I'm going to run it."

Chaos erupted as everyone started talking at once. Charlie gasped. Gretchen squealed. Sabrina and Riley clapped their hands together so loudly, Art jumped.

And this time, Tori was the one to launch herself at Blake. "Do you mean it?"

"I'm not going anywhere." He leaned down and hugged Tori back. "Merry Christmas, niece."

"This is the best gift ever," she mumbled against his shoulder.

"Yeah, not bad." Nadia offered him a fist bump as Tori pulled away. "I mean, it's not a new eyeliner, but it'll do." She grinned.

Charlie's heart swelled with joy. The shelter was safe. Blake was staying, which meant Tori would be staying. It was everything she could have possibly wanted for Christmas.

"The prodigal son returns." Art clapped his hand on Blake's back, his smile threatening to outshine the Christmas tree. "Didn't I tell you?"

Blake winked. "And that's not all."

"What else could there possibly be?" Charlie asked as Blake reached into his pocket for his phone.

He swiped at the screen. "I made an online bulk order after I got off the phone with my boss—estimated delivery in two days."

"For what?" Tori asked, leaning in to see.

Blake turned the phone so they could all view the webpage featuring an image of a colorful package. "Allergy meds."

Everyone burst out laughing.

"This calls for a celebration." Gretchen shot Charlie a pointed look over her shoulder as she waved her hands at the teens and Art. "Everyone, come help me gather more dessert in the kitchen."

Within moments, the living room cleared, leaving Charlie and Blake alone with his presentation still on the screen. She glanced up at it, then at him. Her breath hitched at the look in his eyes.

"I know I tend to rush and push things, but I hope this was a positive exception." He inched closer to her, his gaze holding her hostage. "I had to act fast with my boss. There was no time to waste."

"No, it was absolutely a positive exception." She nodded, her skin tingling at his proximity. "Like Tori said— the best gift ever. In fact, now I feel guilty that I never got you a present."

His expression remained serious despite her nervous grin. "*You're* the gift, Charlie. You and Tori." Blake tugged gently at her arm, and she fell easily into his embrace, as naturally as if she had been born to be there. "I was a fool to have ever left you behind."

She leaned back to see him. "You know I forgive—"

"I know. But I need to say it." His blue gaze roved over hers. "I love you. I did back then, even if I wasn't able to show it properly, and I never stopped."

"I love you, too." Charlie whispered the words in return, the sentiment coming from the deepest part of her heart. She loved Blake—every version of him that she'd known, now meshed into one man she hoped to spend all her future Christmases with.

Blake glanced up, and she followed his gaze to the ceiling. "No mistletoe," she pointed out with a fake pout.

"No problem." His whispered words barely registered before his lips eagerly covered hers. She sank into the kiss, winding her arms around his neck as he pulled her in closer. Her heart soared. This was even better than the mistletoe kiss. That one had been born of confusion and angst and the unresolved past.

This one spoke nothing but sweet promises of the future.

"Merry Christmas, Charlie." Blake wound his fingers into her hair, tucking her against his shoulder.

She let out a contented sigh as she snuggled into his sweater. "Merry Christmas, indeed."

Epilogue

Five months later

"I'm so proud of you." Charlie looped her arms around Blake's waist and smiled up at her new fiancé. "I knew the idea was a good one when I heard it, but it looks like the whole town agrees with me."

Blake rubbed her back, his touch warmer than the May sun streaming across the yard of the recently renovated Jitter Mugs/Paradise Paws combo. "Sometimes I still can't believe I'm here." He grinned down at her, his blue polo accentuating his eyes. Today, they weren't a stormy sea, but a buoyant spring. "And other days, it feels like I never left…Mrs. Bryant."

She slapped at his arm. "Not until June."

"I'm just practicing." He leaned down and kissed her soundly. "We can practice more of that, too."

They kissed again, a lengthy one that filled Charlie's mind with images of white dresses and candelabra and aisles drenched with rose petals.

They stood in contented silence. Charlie ran her finger over the diamond solitaire on her left hand as she and Blake observed the grand opening party happening around them. The dogs—including a few new ones, as several had been recently adopted—ran happily across the lush grass, fetching toys that eager adults and kids alike tossed for them.

Behind them, the original Paradise Paws building had been remodeled and added on to, providing Rachel an office upgrade and a new adjacent space solely for the Jitter Mugs franchise, which featured exclusive Flour Power treats. Blake had even named several of the local menu items after the dogs—Labrador Latte, Mocha Mutt Macchiato and, her personal favorite, Cooper's Cold Brew.

It was all a huge hit.

"Uncle Blake!" Tori rushed up to them, her ponytail swinging as Waffles trotted alongside. Blake had officially adopted Waffles, paying Rachel a small monthly fee to allow the sweet animal to stay on at the rescue until he could have a home with him and Tori. Since finding Tori on Christmas Eve night, Waffles had stuck to her even closer than before. "There you are. I've been looking for you."

"Why is that? Ready for another decaf latte already?" Blake ruffled her hair, and she pretended to be annoyed as she shoved the loose strands back into place. It was all part of their routine, and Charlie loved watching their dynamic develop.

"No, we have a surprise." Tori tugged at his arm, shooting Charlie a pointed look behind his back. *It's time*, she mouthed.

"Right." Charlie rubbed at her chin, hoping to cover the smile she couldn't contain. She'd been ready to burst with this secret for weeks. "Tori and I baked a special congratulations cake for your big grand opening day."

"I would say you didn't have to do that, but I'm glad

you did." He patted his flat stomach and grinned. "What's a party without cake?"

Together, Charlie and Tori led him to the deck off the end of the coffee shop, where patrons could sit and enjoy the view of the water and the dogs as they enjoyed their treats.

"Great party, Blake." Gretchen waved as she and Art climbed the porch steps and joined them at the table in front of the two-tiered cake, along with Nadia, who was carrying a stack of paper plates out the back door of the shop. Blake had hired her as a barista to help her start saving money for college, and so far, she was thriving in her new position, which brought a slice of independence.

Sabrina and Riley had left in March to stay at a foster-to-adopt home in Kansas City. Their departure had been bittersweet—it was good that they were being considered for adoption and got to stay together, which was rare—but it was sad to say goodbye.

And now it was time for another chapter for the rest of them. Charlie handed Tori the cake cutter. "Want to do the honors?"

"This is really nice of you guys. I don't think anyone's made me my own cake before except on my birthday." Blake took a sip of his hazelnut latte that Nadia had whipped up earlier. "I should start new franchises every day."

"Well, this cake is special." Tori slid the cutter carefully into the dessert, then looked up with a grin just as Gretchen snapped a photo on her phone. "It's a gender-reveal cake."

Blake bent over and sputtered coffee. "I'm sorry, *what*?"

"A gender-reveal cake," Tori repeated. She glanced at Charlie, then at Nadia, Gretchen and Art, who grinned widely back at her. They'd been in on the surprise for weeks. She pulled the cutter free of the cake, and pink sprinkles spilled out of the middle. "It's a girl. And it's me."

Blake, who had frozen in place, slowly straightened and set his coffee cup on the table. "Are you saying…"

"I'm ready to move forward with official guardianship." Tori beamed.

"Really?" Blake let out a whoop, pulling her into a bear hug that sent the cake cutter clattering onto the table. "You have no idea what this means to me."

Charlie thought her heart couldn't possibly contain any more happiness until Tori's timid voice spoke, muffled against Blake's shirt. "Can I call you Dad?"

Moisture shone in Blake's eyes as he pulled away, sniffing. "Can I call you Victoria?"

She laughed, her own eyes shining. "Maybe not."

"You can call me anything you want." He ruffled her hair again, and this time Tori didn't even bother to fix it. His eyes met Charlie's, and simultaneously, he and Tori held out their arms. "Get in here, Mrs. Bryant."

"You mean Mom." Tori grinned.

This time, Charlie didn't bother to correct either of them as she joined the group hug—her forever family.

* * * * *

Dear Reader,

I hope you enjoyed reading about the characters of Tulip Mound as much as I enjoyed writing them! As the "dog mom" of a miniature schnauzer named Cooper—yes, he's real!—I knew I had to incorporate some furry canines into my next story.

And I can say, as a Sunday school teacher for the college class at my church, that I also adore teenagers. I might balk at being asked to work in the church nursery, but give me all the teenagers! I love their clever wit, their unique perspective on the world and how they can see things so clearly that adults tend to muddle. I had a blast expressing those characteristics through Tori, Nadia, Sabrina and Riley.

In this novel, I particularly loved the instinctive camaraderie the foster girls felt with the rescue dogs—they had someone who related to feeling left out, rejected and unwanted. Many teenagers struggle with their identity in these ways, even outside the foster system, and could use an adult to remind them of their worth.

I hope in reading *Second Chance Christmas* you'll be blessed, entertained and encouraged—and also that you might consider looking into the wonderful Court Appointed Special Advocates program, CASA, through Volunteers for Youth Justice. Learn more about how to be an advocate for an adolescent in need at vyjla.org/casa/.

Blessings,
Betsy St. Amant

**WE HOPE YOU ENJOYED
THIS BOOK FROM**

LOVE INSPIRED

INSPIRATIONAL ROMANCE

Uplifting stories of faith, forgiveness and hope.

Fall in love with stories where faith helps
guide you through life's challenges, and discover
the promise of a new beginning.

6 NEW BOOKS AVAILABLE EVERY MONTH!

LIHALO2021